THE
SHRINE
AT
ALTAMIRA

JOHN L'HEUREUX

THE
SHRINE
AT
ALTAMIRA

GROVE PRESS
New York

*First published in 1992 by Viking Penguin, a division of Penguin
Books USA Inc.*
Published simultaneously in Canada
Printed in the United States of America

FIRST GROVE PRESS EDITION

Library of Congress Cataloging-in-Publication Data

L'Heureux, John.
    The shrine at Altamira / John L'Heureux.
       p.   cm.
    ISBN 0-8021-3655-9
    I. Title.
    PS3562.H4S47   1999
    813'.54—dc21   99-27591
                           CIP

Designed by Francesca Belanger
Darwing on title page by Anita Kunz

Grove Press
841 Broadway
New York, NY 10003

99 00 01 02   10 9 8 7 6 5 4 3 2 1

For Harriet Doerr

———————

. . . the enigma of cruelty is no more tantalizing than that of the simplest act of love.

ANDRÉ MALRAUX

. . . if you can't imagine yourself an SS officer hustling the Jewish women and children to the gas chamber, you need to be more closely in touch with your buried self.

PAUL FUSSELL

. . . I am seeking the crucial region of the soul where absolute Evil is pitted against fraternity.

ANDRÉ MALRAUX

THE
SHRINE

In a cypress grove just beyond Point Reyes there is a shrine where for centuries survivors of shipwreck, fire, and earthquake have given thanks for their escape from death and, to commemorate their moment of salvation, have offered some token: a piece of driftwood that bore them to shore, the charred blanket that put the fire out, the fallen tile, the shattered glass, sometimes the riven stone itself.

There are no crutches here to show the crippled have been made whole, no abandoned prostheses, no white canes and black glasses. This is not a shrine where miracles occur. It is a place where the faithful come to give thanks, to make vows, to honor life snatched somehow from certain death. There are empty liquor bottles, it is true, and syringes, but no one knows if these are tokens of the saved or the last hope of believers too far gone to pray.

On the trees around the shrine, grateful clients of the Virgin have tacked up vows and letters and poems. As you would expect, they are badly written, often embarrassing and sentimental, and they hint at the secret horrors of lives undone by alcohol, disease, desire, love and lust, and by fate as harsh and impersonal as the winds that blow through Altamira. Without any doubt they are sincere, and all of them, in their way, give thanks. And all of them make promises. All except one. That one, on pale blue paper in a small, neat hand, simply asks a question: "Why?" It is signed *Maria*.

This will be terrible; do not deceive yourself. We hear stories like this on television but we do not look, and when they turn up in newspapers, we glance away, because we know there are crazy people and people who are mad with love, but we refuse to know any more than that. We lead normal lives, careful lives, we are decent men and women.

Still, these things happen.

Still, people do such things.

The shrine at Altamira is ancient, sacred once to gods we no longer recognize, but for the past three hundred years it has been dedicated to the Virgin Mary, Mother of Hope.

ONE

Maria saw Russell for the first time at the Halloween Hop, and she fell in love with him. She was in her junior year and he was a senior, a transfer student, so he didn't know anybody. He was sitting alone, an Anglo, big, and very quiet, and his name was Russell Whitaker. Russell Whitaker, she said to herself. She repeated the name, Russell Whitaker, the sound of money. For fun, and because it was Halloween, she had brought a pair of joke glasses with her, the ones with fuzzy eyebrows and a false nose, and after a while she put on the glasses and went over and stood in front of him.

"Russell Whitaker," she said, "do you want to dance with me?"

He looked up at her, smiled, and then blushed, and said, "I don't dance."

She took off the glasses and stood there.

"I don't know how," he said.

"I could teach you," she said. "Or I could just sit with you."

He looked away, and then he shrugged, so she sat down.

His left hand was twisted a little, and the fingers were smooth and pinkish, as if they weren't real. When he saw her staring, he covered his left hand with his right one.

"My hand," he said.

He had pale blue eyes. Looking into them, she could see he must be very gentle. She leaned close to him. He was wearing Old Spice.

She said nothing, but she was excited and happy.

Until that moment Maria had wanted only one thing: to get away—from her mother and from the purple house and from the rotten neighborhood. To get away from being Mexican-American. To get away from being nobody. But that night at the Halloween Hop, she decided she wanted something else. She wanted Russell Whitaker—who knows why?—and she would get him. She would get away too, but first she would get Russell Whitaker. Everything else could wait.

More than a year passed and they had been lovers for almost that whole time. She was eighteen now, a senior in high school, and Russell was a freshman at San Jose State. He was doing badly, he might flunk out, he was not as smart as she was. But if he flunked out, how would they get away? How would she get away? She thought about this all the time, though she wasn't thinking about it now, because they had just made love and she was lying on her back, waiting for her heart to start beating again. She felt him move in the bed, felt his twisted hand lightly at her breast.

"I've got a job," he said. "I'm going to quit school."

He said, "We can get married."

"Maria?" he said. "What do you think?"

She opened her eyes and smiled at him. "I'm breathing again," she said.

"So what do you think? We can get married now."

It was him she wanted, and she didn't have him yet, not completely. He didn't love her the way she loved him. So when he said again, "We can get married now," she stretched beneath him—thinking Mrs. Russell Whitaker, Maria A. Whitaker—and she said, "Anything. Whatever you want. Only love me," and she twisted her body from beneath his, kissing his shoulder, his neck, his chest.

"Love me," she said, and she fixed him with that look: she made her eyes a little wider as she thought, You are the only thing in the world I'll ever love, and she kept on thinking it until her eyes grew soft and wet, and for that minute he was hers, complete.

"Oh," she said, loving his sudden pain, "love me."

Russell had been sent up to paint the dormer, but as soon as the foreman was out of sight, he scrambled to the top and stood on the peak of the roof, one hand on the chimney for balance. He wanted to get a look at where he was. All around, below him, were rich private homes, with pools and flower gardens and trees everywhere. At a distance, past the freeway and the foothills and the long ridge of mountains, somewhere out there, lay the steely blue of the Pacific Ocean. He stood on the roof, looking. It was another clear winter day in California. Turning a little, he could see the miles and miles of flat-roofed houses, all alike, stretching north and south along El Camino. And he could see the thick cluster of buildings that was San Jose State. He had quit a week ago. He had not waited to flunk out. He turned back to look at the Santa Cruz Mountains, imagining the ocean that lay beyond.

So he was going to marry her. He would move out of the broken-down house he lived in with his father, that drunk, that lunatic, and he would get a little place somewhere that would be their own. He'd be married and have a job and they'd have a life together. They'd be *in* life instead of just watching it. They'd be a couple.

There was something wrong, though, he knew that. He loved Maria, but she loved him more than he loved her. She said so herself. He did love her. He tried to. He just didn't feel it the way he should. But she was almost beautiful, and she was sexy, and when she looked at him the way she did sometimes, he knew she was the right one for him. When she looked at him, he had a feeling that he *was* somebody. Was that the same as being in love? And who else would have him anyway?

He took off his cap—a white painter's cap, stiff,

not yet shaped to his head—and wiped his forehead with it and then put it back on. He looked over at San Jose State.

Maybe he should wait until he fell in love with somebody the way Maria was in love with him. Because, after all, what was the rush? He could go on living with his father; he wasn't afraid of him anymore, and his father knew it. He didn't have to worry about any crap from him. He could save money, and wait. It was scary to get married and have your own place to live and somebody to support. But he would never find anybody better than Maria. And he wanted something to happen.

He wanted to make something happen.

He looked out toward the mountains, but he was seeing her face beneath him as they made love. "Russell," she said, like magic, like casting a spell. He repeated it now, standing on the roof, saying it the way she said it to him, in bed, in love. He saw her face. "Love me," she said, adoring, sexy. "Love me."

"Hey, peckerhead," the foreman shouted. "You're supposed to be painting that dormer."

Russell waved at him and began edging down the slope of the roof to the dormer. It was his second week and he was still not comfortable with heights.

"Sometime today!" the foreman yelled, and went to check on the others.

Russell stood on the scaffolding now and stared into the bucket of paint. He sniffed and wiped his nose

with the back of his hand. He hated the smell of paint.
This was going to be his life from now on, for good.

Between history and English periods Maria was standing at her locker, pretending to look for a book. Actually, she was thinking and didn't want anybody to
see her doing it. It had just struck her once again, at
the end of history period, that sex and love and marriage were completely different things and the other
kids didn't seem to know it. She knew it, and she knew
what she was getting into. She'd marry, which would
be one kind of life, and then she'd finish high school
and win a scholarship and go to college, which would
be another kind of life, but she'd be Mrs. Whitaker
by then, with a husband who was a housepainter, and
this is where it got too complicated for her. She'd miss
the fun of college, and dates, and late nights in the
dorms. She'd miss being young and free like the others.
Her life really wouldn't be her own. But she loved
Russell, she wanted him, she wanted to marry him.
Why?

She stopped thinking and leaned her head against
the locker door.

Why should she marry him? The question kept coming back to her, stupidly. She loved him, that's why.
She pulled herself up straight. She had to think.

She stared into her locker, thinking.

Somebody was standing behind her, but she didn't
turn to look. To hell with them. She bent over and
searched through the books and crap on the floor of

her locker as if she expected to find something she'd lost. She stood up. They were still there. She turned around to face whoever it was. She was ready with her fighting look.

It was Marcy Sherman, whose father owned the Sherman department stores, and she gave Maria that thin smile of hers and said, "I was looking at your hair. You have the most beautiful hair I've ever seen."

Maria stared hard at her and saw she wasn't joking or being mean or putting her on.

"Like silk," Marcy said.

Maria softened. She drew a strand of hair through her fingers, looking at it, and then she looked at Marcy. For that minute, she couldn't speak. The bell rang. "Time for class," Maria said, and tried to smile.

But she did not go to English class. She went down the corridor to the girls' room where she locked the stall door and, huddling against the back wall, she cried. She didn't know why.

For the hell of it, just playing a game, Maria told Russell she would not marry him. "I've changed my mind," she said. "I can't go through with it."

She had been doing this, off and on, for the entire month since he'd first asked her. She explained herself differently each time.

A month ago she had said yes, she would marry him, but the circumstances were different then—they had just finished making love and his eyes were so soft and pleading that of course she had said yes—so it didn't count. The next day she had decided not to marry him. She wanted more than he could give her, she said, she wanted out and *up*. She didn't want to be a painter's wife. Besides, she had taken the SATs and might get a scholarship. She couldn't give up her future. She had to have a life too. Russell was crushed and for days he wandered around in a deep depression, attentive as always but saying almost nothing. Then one afternoon he showed up at her house and he was furious. He could barely speak, and he looked mad enough to strike her, so she gave him a glass of iced tea and told him to have a seat and calm down. He sat there at the kitchen table, staring, squeezing the glass, hard. There was a sudden popping sound as the tumbler shattered in his hand, a tinkle of glass, and then tea flooded the cloth and there was blood on his palm. So she said yes after all, she would marry him. She wanted him, more than anything in the world. She gave him that look. He was elated.

A week later she said no, and once more he was depressed. But the next day she got her SAT scores, and they were very bad. She could forget about Stanford or Harvard or Yale, she could see that, and maybe about every other place as well. What if she couldn't get in anywhere? What if she just didn't have it? She burned the College Board letter and told her friends Michelle and Benni that her scores were 740 Verbal and 699 Math. She told Russell yes, she would marry him, yes, again. And again he was elated.

A few days later, resentful that she was sacrificing

college for marriage, she told him no, and watched while his dumb anger set in and he grew silent and furious and powerless, and then she said she was only teasing. Yes, she would marry him.

She didn't know why she did this, except that it was a wonderful game, wanting him and pretending not to want him—Russell Whitaker with his pale blue eyes. It was terrible to do this to him. She was simply terrible, she told her friend Michelle, the way she tortured him with her love.

Mrs. Russell Whitaker, she thought. Maria A. Whitaker.

Later, a full month since she first agreed to marry him, Maria said for the last time, "I've made up my mind. I can't do it."

There was silence for a moment, and then a remarkable thing happened. Something in Russell changed.

Maria saw the change as it happened. She had just refused him, and she watched as his jaw went rigid and a red flush mounted from his neck to his ears, and his pale eyes narrowed in fury. Then slowly the blood drained from his face and she thought he was going to faint, but he only stared at her, speechless, white, his eyes nearly closed. This wasn't like his usual anger; he looked sick; he looked like he might die. She put her hand on his arm. His skin was wet and cold. There was an acid smell to him. She wanted to run and hide, but she waited, her hand on his arm, and gradually his color returned. He opened his eyes.

After a moment, he shook his head a little and smiled at her as if nothing had happened. He loved her, he said, he couldn't live without her, he was crazy for her.

She had no idea what had happened to him, or to them, but she decided she would not play that game anymore.

Seven years from now, in jail awaiting sentence, Russell would think of this moment and smile bitterly, because he understood at last what had happened to him. He had fallen in love. The balance had shifted, and he loved Maria more than she loved him. At that moment he had loved her so badly he wanted to kill her.

Sitting in his jail cell, waiting, Russell would think of her and smile, and sometimes he would laugh—a short, harsh bark with no pleasure in it. At these times his cellmate was moved to strike a match and toss the burning flame at him, halfheartedly, a reminder, just to keep him on his toes.

It was a beautiful winter morning—not a hint of rain—and Ana Luisa was on her way to Blackberry Heights in Los Altos to clean house for the Jacobsons.

Ana Luisa cleaned house for nine families in the San Jose area, one house in the morning and one in the afternoon, five days a week, with Friday afternoon off. She made a good living. The women she cleaned for thought she was the old-fashioned kind. And, mostly, she was. She wore a scarf on her head and tattered espadrilles on her feet, and she pretended to understand only a little English and to speak none at all. *"Sí,"* she answered, *"sí, sí,"* to whatever they asked her to do, and then she was free to ignore them or not, depending on how she felt. And what could they do about it? Cleaning women were not easy to find.

In other ways, of course, she was not old-fashioned. She liked to dance and she liked men. Her ankles were getting thick, and her waist too, but her breasts were still fine and she was still young enough and good-looking enough to go dancing Saturdays and pick up her share of men. She could have another husband anytime she wanted one, but who would want one? Men were good for only one thing, and that was the truth. She thought of her Paco and how proud he was of his big *cosa,* down to his knees almost. It was the only thing about him that she missed.

She blessed herself; she was a weak woman. She would rather die than have Maria know some of the thoughts she had, let alone the things she did on those Saturday nights. She should make a pilgrimage, filthy sinner that she was, no better than a whore. Well, a little better. A lot. She should go back to the shrine at Altamira.

She had gone there once, right after the fire, and in many ways she dated the beginning of her life from that time. Paco had died in the fire—half the trailer camp had died—but she and Maria had survived. For no reason. It was a miracle. She had thanked the Virgin, leaving at the shrine a little silver crucifix she'd worn as a necklace, and then she set about building herself a new life.

Her picture had been on the television: her dress torn, the baby in her arms, she stood dazed and beautiful among the ashes of the trailer camp. When she returned from Altamira and went to City Hall for aid, she found a packet of letters from people who had seen her on TV. There were offers of money and blankets and—best of all—the offer of a job with Your Third Hand Housecleaners. She took the job at once, and all the overtime she could get. In a year she left the agency and went to work for herself.

She had done well. She had a big Chevy, a junker, that she drove back and forth to work, and she had a nice little house, cement blocks painted a good grayish-purple color, with petunias in the front yard and an old tree in the back, and a low fence that kept dogs from running through her flowers. The neighborhood was bad, people said, but it seemed okay to her. There were a lot of drunks around, and those teenage kids in the summer, but you could expect drunks and wild kids anywhere, and if drugs were sold on her street, she didn't know about it. So she figured she had done well for herself. And for Maria.

Maria had her own room and big ideas, too big maybe, but she was going to get out of here and go to college and have a better life. Maria was different from her; she wanted other things, Anglo things, and she was afraid of nothing.

THE SHRINE AT ALTAMIRA

For Ana Luisa the thought of going away to college—just being with all those rich kids and the way they did things always right and never having fun—it was enough to make her thankful that she herself was just a cleaning woman. She scrubbed toilets and tiles and vacuumed thick rugs in their houses, but she did not have to be with them or live like them and she thanked God for that, and the Virgin. She was lucky to be just herself.

In this way, too, she was old-fashioned: she knew it was the Virgin who was responsible for her good luck. She had always been lucky. And pretty too. In her living room, and never mind what Maria said about it, she kept a little shrine to the Virgin. Her statue stood in a plaster grotto made to look like stone, with a sort of altar in front of her where Ana Luisa placed a vigil candle at special times, and around the sides were family pictures and some postcards and three mementos Ana Luisa never talked about: a shell and two small stones.

She smiled to herself as she pulled into the circular drive at the Jacobsons'. When Maria graduated in June, they would go back to Altamira, and together they would thank the Virgin for their good luck.

She parked the car and sat for a moment, gathering her strength for the morning ahead. Three toilets, two bedrooms, the family room, the kitchen floor and counters, a little dusting, and she would be done. The house was new. If Mrs. Jacobson left her alone, she'd be out of there by eleven. Then she could go to the shopping mall and get something nice, something pretty, for Maria.

Maria had followed directions with great care, and there was no doubt about it, she was pregnant. She stood, staring at the tiny dish as the stuff in it turned from white to pink, and for just a second she felt thrilled, powerful. She was going to be a mother, she was going to give birth to a son. She knew it was a boy. She could feel it. But a second later her excitement gave way to something else, a vague dread, a kind of guiltiness. She should have an abortion; that's what her friends would do. They'd get rid of the baby, and then cry about it, and after a while they'd joke about it in the girls' room, and pretty soon it would all be over. They'd go on to college and never think of it again. But her mother would kill her if she had an abortion. And besides, who cared what her friends thought? They weren't her. They weren't living her life. She was. And she'd live it her way.

The next day, in English class, she tried to call back those first feelings of excitement and power, but they escaped her now. Nonetheless, she told herself, she was glad she was having a baby. She would marry Russell. She would be a mother. A mom.

"Maria?" the teacher said.

Maria looked up and saw that the other kids were all staring at her. This was the second time her name had been called, and everybody was ready for the big laugh.

"I'm sorry," Maria said, "I wasn't listening."

The teacher, for once, had nothing sarcastic to say. He raised his hand to his forehead as if he had a headache, and then he lowered it, saying softly, "What is the use? Why even bother?"

Maria ignored him. She wouldn't have to put up with this kind of humiliation ever again. She was choosing her own life. She was choosing what she wanted.

It was an hour since Maria had kissed Russell goodbye. She aired her room as soon as he left, but it still smelled of lovemaking, and so she lit an incense candle they kept for the living room shrine, and set the candle on her bureau. She had not told Russell about the baby. But she would have to tell her mother. Now.

Maria showered and put on a Sunday dress—a Mexican blouse with ruffles and a full skirt—and though she usually wore lipstick, she made sure there was no trace of it on her mouth this afternoon. She examined herself in the mirror, trying to see what her mother would see. She fluffed her hair out in curls. "God," she said, but left it that way. Her mother would like it.

"I'm getting married," she said into the mirror. "I'm pregnant." She shook her head.

Pinned to the wall above her bureau were snapshots

of girls in her class, and a school pennant, and the joke glasses she had hung there on the night of the Halloween Hop. The glasses had a false nose attached, and wild furry eyebrows, and for no reason at all she put them on and looked into the mirror. "I'm getting married," she said. "I'm pregnant." She reached behind her ears and made the glasses waggle up and down. She felt a queasiness in her stomach, a momentary nausea spasm, and then everything was fine again. "I'm very happy," she said.

She was still standing at the mirror when she heard the car pull up in front of the house. She took off the glasses. She went to the living room and looked around quickly to make sure it was tidy. She sniffed at the doorway to her bedroom. The air seemed all right now—that sourish smell of sex was gone—and so she brought the incense candle into the living room and set it down before the shrine.

She looked out the window. Her mother was getting out of the car, gathering up her string bag and a sack of groceries, and God knows what else. Why was she so slow? Maria wanted it all to be over, the shouting and the fighting and the tearful reconciliation, the whole ethnic mess.

"Mama," she said, holding open the door for her mother.

"*Qué bonita,*" Ana Luisa said, "*Qué adorable te ves,*" but she saw Maria's look and said, "Okay, no Spanish, *querida,* not tonight. I've got the nicest chicken for our dinner. Plump, but not a lot of fat.

Like me. Take this, Maria," and she put the grocery bag into Maria's arms. She turned to make the sign of the cross before the shrine, and at once she saw the burning candle.

"What is this?" she said. She stepped over to the kitchen door. "What's happened?"

"Nothing's happened," Maria said. She continued to take things from the bag and put them in the cupboard. "I just thought you'd like to see the candle lit in front of the shrine."

Ana Luisa said nothing.

Maria folded the bag and stooped to put it in the cabinet under the sink. She was determined to control this situation, so she stood up slowly and turned toward her mother with a defiant look.

"What, Maria?" Ana Luisa whispered, taking Maria by surprise.

Her mother was helpless, Maria saw. Her mother was completely at her mercy. At once all the hardness in Maria melted and she threw herself into Ana Luisa's arms, sobbing.

Ana Luisa held her close. She knew. Maria was pregnant.

"Oh, Mama, I'm so scared."

"It's all right. Everything will be all right."

They held each other, hard. After a moment, Maria pulled away from her and said, "I'm going to get married."

Ana Luisa nodded, but she said, "No, Maria. No, *querida*."

"*Sí,* Mama," Maria said. And then she edged past her and disappeared into the bathroom.

Ana Luisa stood in the doorway, her face hard, expressionless. The baby would have to go, that much was certain. Maria had her whole life ahead of her, and she would not let her throw it away because of one mistake. She heard Maria throw up, she heard the toilet flush, but she was not listening. She was thinking, Here it is, my life all over again. A little fun, a dance maybe, kissing in the car, his hand on your breasts or the inside of your thigh, a few minutes letting him have his way, and then you're pregnant and married and your life is over. After that, it's all fighting and drunkenness, with a few sweaty nights of love. That's it. You spend the next forty years scrubbing gringo toilets so your daughter can have a better life. You pretend you don't even speak English, you put up with their shit and their shitty wages and their contempt, and what's it all for?

Sometimes she felt she could curse God.

Instead, she poured herself a tumbler of red wine and stood at the sink drinking it. She heard Maria go to her bedroom and shut the door behind her and she thought of going in after her and telling her a thing or two. Laying down the law. As long as you are in my house, you'll do as I say. You're not getting married, *niña,* and you're not going to have that baby. Who is the father anyway? *I* don't know him. No boys ever come here. Then a thought struck her like a fist at her heart. Maybe *Maria* didn't know who the father was. Her daughter playing the whore? She pressed her hand against her breast and drained the glass of wine.

She must be very calm. She must be reasonable. She poured herself another tumbler of wine. No screaming and swearing. No wild threats. No giving in to the temptation to beat her senseless, the little fool, the little whore. Whore of a whore, it was always the same.

When she'd drained half the tumbler, Ana Luisa pulled herself up straight and, ready for business, went over to the shrine and knelt down, heavily. She said an Ave kneeling upright and had started in on a second one, when suddenly it all seemed hopeless, and she sat back on her heels and groaned. She looked up into the pink face of the Virgin and said, "Help me." She let her bosom slump forward comfortably. "It's my Maria," she said. *"Socórrame."*

She knelt there for quite a while, her heels grinding into her buttocks and her knees killing her, while she let her mind wander back to Paco, how handsome he was when they first met, and how they had made love in the bushes and in his mother's house—that terrible old *bruja*—and once even in broad daylight down by the railroad tracks. A train had gone by, but they'd kept right on and Paco never missed a stroke. When you were young . . . She made the sign of the cross and asked the Virgin to forgive her, she was such a whore, and help her daughter Maria because it was not too late yet. Maybe she could have a miscarriage. Maybe she could be crossing the street and get hit by a truck, only gently, gently, so that she wouldn't have even a bad bruise, but she would lose the baby. These things happened sometimes. Was it too much to ask?

She continued to kneel, praying, and then her mind wandered again, and she found herself thinking that the greatest miracle would be if Maria wasn't pregnant at all. She tried to remember what Maria had said. She had said she was scared. She had said she was getting married. But she hadn't said she was pregnant, had she? Ana Luisa felt her heart lift for a moment. Could it be? Another miracle? Girls knew things these days. It wasn't like in her day, when all you had were those rubber safeties that no real man would even buy. Maybe marriage was just a crazy idea Maria had picked up after she did badly in those college exams. *"Ay, Virgen Santísima . . ."* she began, and almost at once she was on her feet and tapping at Maria's door.

"Querida?" she said. "It's Mama."

Maria was lying on her bed, but she sat up as her mother opened the door and came in. She got up and stood on the far side of the bed next to the bureau.

"It's *Mamacita,"* Ana Luisa said. She could see Maria was expecting the worst. "No fights, *querida,* no screaming or anything. Listen, how low I'm keeping my voice. You can't even hear me. *Sí?"*

"I'm getting married," Maria said.

"Sí, sí, my little one, but not now. Later, when you're older and you've graduated from high school, and maybe college, and you meet some nice boy, one of our own kind but with a good job and very handsome and—"

"I'm pregnant," Maria said.

Ana Luisa's heart stopped. Her breath stopped. She expected any minute to drop dead.

She watched as Maria turned away from her to the bureau and picked up those glasses with the false nose and the fuzzy eyebrows. She watched, stupid, as Maria put them on and looked at herself in the mirror and then turned back to her and said again, "I'm pregnant. I'm getting married."

She took a step toward Maria and, numb with anger, she felt her hand rise from her side and crack down hard against the girl's face, catching her on the left cheek and sending the glasses spinning into the air and across the room. It happened so quickly that neither of them moved. Maria stood there—her face raised to her mother's hand, and the hand suspended in the air—as if what had just been done could never be undone, and they would hold these positions for all eternity.

It was Ana Luisa who cried out, a sharp piercing wail, half fury and half despair, as she grabbed Maria's shoulders and shook her and shook her. *"Puta! Puta!"* she screamed as Maria fought against her, and suddenly she had Maria by the hair and was pushing her and then dragging her from the bedroom to the living room, where she threw her to her knees before the shrine. Ana Luisa's screaming gave way to tears finally and she looked around, confused, and then fell to her knees beside her sobbing daughter. "Dear Virgin in heaven," she said, "forgive me," and she threw her arms around Maria and wept.

Maria collapsed against her, grateful, because she knew how these things went. The scene was nearly done, and in a while they could be reconciled, and in the end, after all the screaming and crying and making up, nothing at all would be changed.

"It was pure ethnic," Maria said, "you should have seen it. She'd had some wine, of course, to get her energy up, and she was screaming 'Whore' at me, and slapping me around, and then she dragged me out to the shrine—can you believe it?—she *dragged* me, like by the hair, like this was some kind of movie or something? Then she collapsed and started hugging me, and saying, 'Holy Virgin, forgive me,' and stuff like that, because she was getting tired, I suppose, and she figured she'd better make up with me while she still had the strength left to do it. God, that woman!"

Russell listened and said nothing. He had picked Maria up after work and they'd driven to San Gregorio Beach, where they were parked now, sitting in the car, facing out over the ocean. Rain beat hard against the windshield, making it impossible for them to see, but they could hear the crash of the waves below them. The place seemed right for their mood. They huddled together against all the noise.

"It was an incredible scene," Maria said. "Pure ethnic."

"She loves you, I guess."

"Well, of course she loves me. But what a way to show it. What a way to, you know, carry on. Other families don't live like that. It's something in their culture, Mexicans; it makes me ashamed to be one. They have to scream and yell about everything. They're insane. They're simply insane. I wish I had blue eyes, like yours."

He moved his hand higher and could feel the swell of her breast. He touched it gently with one finger, caressing it. He was not aroused. He was hollowed out, empty of everything except this ache, this need for her. To be with her. To hold her.

"If we have a baby, I hope he has your eyes."

"We won't have a baby."

"Everybody has babies," she said.

He felt a knot tighten in his stomach, or maybe it was in his heart.

"What?" she said. "Don't you want babies at all?"

"I want you," he said, pulling her close, holding her so hard that she could barely breathe. "I don't want anything or anybody else. Just you." He pressed his mouth down upon hers, his teeth cutting into her lip, her tongue, and he seemed to be gasping for air, as if he could draw her breath into his lungs and thus possess her. She shifted her body so that they could make love, and she reached down to touch him. But he brushed her hand away. It was not sex he was after. It was something else, beyond sex.

"What?" she said, whispering. "Russell, what?"

"I want *you*," he said.

It was a voice she did not recognize. She stared into his pale blue eyes and saw what looked like steel, but as she continued to stare, she saw only emptiness. She was frightened at first, and then excited, and then filled with a completely new feeling, a kind of power. She laughed.

They made love, fierce and hard, like animals in heat, and then they rested, separate again, looking out through the rain at the broken ocean beyond.

"Let's get married soon," he said.

She smiled, content, and said nothing.

Russell had begun once more to gnaw at the dry flesh of his little finger, something he hadn't done in years. The skin was hard and flaky, as if there were only bone beneath it and no flesh at all. He had been doing this since the night she refused him, and he'd had that fit, and then she never refused him again.

They were going to get married and the girl didn't even know him, she didn't even know who he was. He was Russell Whitaker, an Anglo with a nice Anglo name, and that's all she wanted to know. He had been thinking of this for days and wishing he could do something about it. He resolved to tell her now, tonight.

They had been to the Old Mill for a double feature—*Rocky* I and II, or maybe it was III and IV; he couldn't remember—and then they'd driven in silence to Skyline Lookout, where they were going to park and make love, but she was very quiet tonight, distracted almost, and so they didn't make love. He was glad not to. They just sat there in silence, her head nestled in the crook of his shoulder, his right arm cradling her, and his right hand resting softly against her breast. He wanted to tell her, and now was the perfect time. The pressure had been building in him for weeks—to tell her, to come out with it—as if there were another person inside him who wanted to get out. He decided he would do it now, he would do it now, he would do it now, but they continued to sit there in silence, until finally she whispered, "What?" and, grateful, overwhelmed with love and trust, he held out before her his left hand. It was pink, deformed, the fingers more like a plastic glove than like flesh and bone.

She had asked him about it that night at the Halloween Hop, and he had told her it happened when he was just a kid, five or six years old. A bunch of them were playing around a fire and two of the older kids dared him to pour a can of Quik Start on the flames and he did it. The can exploded, turning his hand into a kind of torch, and . . . well, this is what happened. He had told the same story to the doctor who treated his hand, and he had told it many times over the years since the accident. He told it so well he almost believed it himself.

But now, for once, he wanted to say the truth and let her know him. He held out his hand so she could see it in all its ugliness—pink, slick, deformed. He turned the words over and over in his mind—My father did this—but no words came out, and before he could force them out, she lifted the hand to her lips and kissed it. He sucked in his breath, he choked, and she turned the hand over and kissed the hard smooth palm.

He wanted to crush her into his body, he wanted to enter her and fill her full of him until they were only one person, he wanted . . . but what did he want?

She placed his deformed hand between her breasts and held it there. She smiled at him.

He could never tell her now.

"We have to talk about the wedding," Ana Luisa said, looking up from her ironing. "We've got to make preparations."

"I'm doing my homework," Maria said. "On Sunday we'll talk about it."

"If you had spent every night doing homework . . . ," Ana Luisa said, and left the thought suspended.

Maria made a show of not listening.

She and Russell were getting married on Saturday, at City Hall, so her Sunday talk with her mother would never have to take place. She felt bad about excluding her mother, but what could she do? The woman simply wasn't reasonable, and Maria was damned if she was going to have a Catholic wedding: going to the priest for instructions, making her confession, and then the Mexican fiesta with bridesmaids and pink dresses and tuxedos and everybody drunk. And for what? To prove she had a man and was not going to college and would never get out of this place? To prove she was a good Mexican girl? Fuck it all. She was going to get married at City Hall on Saturday, honeymoon until Sunday night, and go to school on Monday morning. Marriage was not the end of her life; it was a stop on the way. Her mother would just have to get used to that.

"A nice white dress," Ana Luisa said, "with the bridesmaids all in pink. Or in different colors each one, whatever you like."

"Mama!"

"I'm just thinking ahead," she said, deftly maneuvering the iron under and over the ruffles of Maria's blouse. "We'll talk about it Sunday. *Muy bien.*"

They were happy. They walked along the beach hand in hand, an innocent young couple in love. They had been married the day before, they would be together now forever and ever, they would never be apart.

Mr. and Mrs. Russell Whitaker.

There was nothing more that either of them wanted. They had each other. They had everything.

They were married and in love. They were happy.

They were living in sin, Ana Luisa thought, but they were so happy and so adorable, who could say it was wrong? They came over every evening for dinner, and afterward as they watched television—she in her chair, Maria and Russell on the couch—she spent more time looking at them than at the TV. They were so cute.

Maria was in her third month and hadn't begun to show yet, but she had filled out a little in the face, and her breasts were larger, and she had that look some women get when they're pregnant, as if they're concealing some wonderful secret. And, for sure, Maria had a secret—she hadn't yet told Russell about the baby. What was she waiting for? Russell would be glad to be a father; he'd like it. Some men did, and anybody could see Russell was manly without being macho like a fool. He'd be gentle with a baby. She looked over at him, sitting there with an arm around Maria's shoulder, her head nestled against his cheek. Such a cute picture. Russell was big, six feet at least, and maybe two hundred pounds. Even with that burned left hand, he would know how to please a woman, she said to herself, and for a moment she could feel his weight on top of her. What an idea! What a whore she was! No wonder her daughter had married outside the Church. No wonder they were living in sin. She made a tiny sign of the cross and forced herself to concentrate on the TV.

Maria nudged Russell in the ribs. Her mother had just made the sign of the cross, furtively, which meant she must be thinking about them again. Living in sin. Her mother was old school; what could you do? Maria herself felt free of all that: free of the Church and its rules and superstitions, free of her mother's old-fashioned ideas, and free of this house and this neighborhood and of being Mexican. Hispanic, they called it now, but it meant the same thing—second class. She and Russell had their own place, a trailer, but at least it was a home of their own. She carried a key to her old house, a key to her new one, and a key to their car, a three-year-old Ford, not a big old junker like her mother's. Some mornings she dropped Russell off at his job and then drove the car to school, like a working woman, only different. At school she was now Maria Whitaker. She was practically an Anglo herself. And she was going to have a baby. The baby would make a big difference in their lives, so she had decided not to tell Russell until she had to. He was in love with her, but she wasn't sure how much. He wasn't ready to hear about any baby yet. She shifted closer to him on the couch. She put her hand on his lap, palm up, and he put his left hand in hers. She could feel his dick move the tiniest bit beneath the back of her hand. She pressed down a little and moved her hand forward and then back. At once she could feel him begin to get hard. She giggled, and he crossed his legs, moving her hand away, embarrassed in front of Ana Luisa. They all continued to stare at the screen. So far as she was concerned, Maria thought, life could go on like this forever. She loved him, and he loved her more and more—he acted silly sometimes just to make her laugh—and the other things, like college and a good job and everything else, didn't seem to matter anymore. Because in a way she had escaped already. At school they all envied her. And she had begun to like the idea of being a mother. She rubbed the tough pink skin of his hand with her own perfect fingers, and she sighed. Mrs. Russell Whitaker.

Russell leaned harder against Maria so she would feel his weight and know he was there beside her. He was not going to look at her until the next commercial. He rationed his looks, because each of them mattered and because what he saw in her eyes allowed him to get through the boredom of his day. Standing on a roof or a scaffolding or a ladder—always balanced somewhere, half expecting to fall—he would feel like tossing his brush to the ground and taking off, but instead he would turn away from the paint, take a deep breath, and think of her. In a minute he was able to go on. He hated painting, he hated the smell of the stuff, but at the end of the day he would have Maria, and then he could be happy. He had never been in love before. He'd had sex, once, in his sophomore year of high school, with a girl who wanted to feel his hand in the dark, and though she said the sex was fantastic, he had only felt bad. At her insistence, they tried it again to see if the second time might be better. But he hadn't felt anything for her either time. "Doesn't it just feel *good?*" she asked, and he didn't know what she meant. Sex was not the same as love, he knew that much, and he had never loved anybody. He had never even liked anybody. Could that be true? Even before the accident to his hand? He could re-member only Billy Muir, with his high voice and his little short pants that were always too small for him.

They had played together every day. But after Russell's accident, Billy was never allowed to play with him again, though he came over once to borrow a sack of marbles—or were they Indian beads?—and never gave them back. Sitting here watching television with his wife and his mother-in-law, Russell ached for the little boy he had been. It was cruel to do that to a child, isolate him, refuse to let your children play with him. It was punishing the victim a second time. Because of course they must have realized it was not an accident, that his father had simply grabbed his hand and held it to the flames. Everybody knew his father was a drunk. Russell felt the anger building in him, the taste of rust in his mouth, despair, and despite himself he turned to look at Maria, and she looked back, and he was saved.

He saw in her eyes that he was loved and he did not, finally, have to die.

At lunch hour Maria and Michelle walked down to the practice field where they could sit on the bleachers and talk in private. Everybody wanted to be Maria's friend now that she was pregnant, but she remained faithful to Michelle and Jennifer, who had been her friends since grammar school. Jennifer had cheerleading practice during lunch, which was nice, because it gave Maria a chance to talk about everything twice.

"Are you still not throwing up?" Michelle asked. "By now you should be throwing up all the time."

"I never throw up," Maria said.

"Do you have pains at least? You should feel nauseous and everything."

"I feel fine. I haven't had morning sickness once."

"I don't see how you can be in your third month and not have morning sickness," Michelle said. "My sister just had a kid, and for the first three months she threw up all the time. She was like a barf machine. She'd get up in the morning and . . . oooops, up it came. It was like a fountain or something. I'd hear her in the bathroom, and I'd think, Jesus, I'm never gonna have a kid. Barf city."

"Do you mind, Michelle? Like I'm eating?"

"That's another thing. You're supposed to throw up before meals all the time. No shit. What does your doctor say? Who do you go to anyway? Is it a man or a woman?"

"Can we stop talking about this? Please?"

"Sorry. Touchy, touchy. You *are* in your third month."

Maria said nothing for a while, and then she said, "I haven't seen a doctor."

Michelle looked at her, and looked away, and then looked back. "Are you serious? You mean you went just by the home test kit?" She waited. "You did, didn't you. You just used the home test kit. Maybe you didn't do it right. You know?" She drew in her breath sharply. "My God, maybe you aren't pregnant at all."

Maria folded the plastic wrap around her half-eaten

sandwich and stuffed it back into the bag. She stood up and brushed crumbs off her skirt.

"You should see a doctor right away, Maria. Or at least the school nurse." She put her hand on Maria's arm. "Maybe you married him when you didn't even have to."

Maria pulled her arm away and started up the hill toward school.

"Well, you don't have to be mad at *me,*" Michelle said, following behind.

"Leave me alone," Maria said.

"Well, it's insane to get married because you're pregnant when you aren't even sure about it."

Maria rounded on her. "I married him because I love him, and I would've married him even if I wasn't pregnant, but I am pregnant, so just leave me alone." She turned away from Michelle. "The truth is you're just jealous."

She continued on up the hill. She was fed up with high school kids. Those idiots. Those assholes.

Russell and Maria were on their way to Ana Luisa's for dinner. Two days earlier Maria had gotten the doctor's report: she was not pregnant, nor had there ever been any reason to think she was. It had taken her this long to accept the fact.

"Russell?" she said, putting her hand on his leg.

He put his hand on hers and squeezed it. For some reason, she had been very affectionate these last two days. She had said little, but she was all over him and he liked it.

"I'm not pregnant," she said. "I'm not going to have a baby."

"Good," he said, and looked at her. "That's a relief."

She took her hand off his leg and shifted away from him on the front seat.

He began to whistle.

When they arrived, Ana Luisa took one look at them and concluded that the honeymoon was over. Marriage, she thought, it's just another form of hell.

Russell and Bog were painting a seven-room pool house in Atherton, and the super had left to check on another job, so they sat down by the pool and Bog broke out the Camels. Russell shook his head, no.

"This is the life," Bog said, getting comfortable in the chaise longue. The pool had a black bottom that made the water look like ink. "Look at that water."

Russell had been looking at the water. Since he first saw it this morning he had been thinking how good it would be to walk down those steps into the water and never come up again.

"So how's married life?" Bog said. "Free nooky all the time . . . I envy you. I'll tell you, though, you don't look like you're getting much. You look like you're getting shit."

Russell gave him a sour look. "What do you know

about marriage, Bog? What do you know about *life?* Jesus."

For the past week Maria had scarcely spoken to him. When he asked her why, she would say, "Figure it out," or "Go to hell," or "You make me sick." He was waiting for her to come around and tell him what was the matter, what he had done wrong, but he was tired of waiting and he wanted to make something happen. He had felt the rage building in him all week.

"So I guess you're not getting any," Bog said, and flipped his lighted cigarette into the black water.

At once Russell was out of his chair and leaning over Bog. He grabbed him by the shirtfront and, with one powerful yank, got him up out of the chaise longue and onto his feet. Bog wavered a little, and Russell pitched him headlong into the water. There was a splash, and then Bog surfaced, sputtering. "What're you, crazy?" he shouted. "Are you out of your fucking mind?"

Russell stepped to the tile border of the pool and said quietly, "Don't throw cigarettes in the water."

Bog had one hand up, ready to hoist himself out of the water, but Russell loomed over him still. Bog put his other hand up, waiting. Russell did not move. "What?" Bog said. Russell pressed his foot gently against the top of Bog's head. He held it there, pressing harder. Then harder. Bog ducked away and, carefully, moved back in the water. He looked up at him. He saw that Russell's eyes were dead and his face had no expression at all. He looked very, very dangerous.

"Let me out of here," Bog said.

There was a long silence while Russell stood above him, looking, and then he said, "I get what I need, Bog. Don't you worry about me."

Maria hadn't spoken to Russell for a week. But for the next week she worked hard at trying to cheer him up, win him over, make him laugh a little. She had forgotten how much fun it was to try and please him. Besides, she needed him if she was going to get pregnant. As the days passed she discovered once again that Russell was what she wanted and that pursuing him was fun. It was fun and it was easy.

"Listen," she said. "I'm going to learn to cook. Then we won't have to go to Mama's all the time."

They were sitting in McDonald's, having the Big Mac Combo. She put down her Big Mac and started to wipe her fingers on her napkin, but instead she reached over and put a dot of ketchup on the tip of Russell's nose.

"What do you think?" she said.

Russell stuck his tongue out, trying to get the ketchup, and he crossed his eyes and lowered his head to the table. Maria laughed, delighted. He slipped low in the booth until only his head showed, and finally his head disappeared and he was under the table. Maria giggled, and then she laughed, and then she let out a little shout of surprise as his head burrowed between her legs. She pushed him away, laughing, and in a moment he came up from beneath the table and was sitting beside her. "Disgusting," someone said, but Russell and Maria ignored whoever it was and went on snuggling in the booth. Together they ate her Big Mac and then they ate his. She had forgotten how good their good times were.

Afterward, in the car, Maria said, "I've got this *Sunset* cookbook and they explain everything? With pictures of what it's supposed to look like, you know, when it's halfway done and then when it's all done? Chicken in a white sauce and coq au vin. Flank steak. Everything. It looks like anybody could do it. So what do you think?"

"Well, hell, why not? Maybe I could learn too, and do it when you don't feel like it, or just to surprise you?"

"I want to do it for *you*," she said.

Russell gave that little gulping sound he made—half gratitude and half passion—and, putting his arm around her, he pulled her close. She settled against him, her hand on his knee, her arm resting on his thigh. They drove in silence, very happy.

That night they lay in bed, quiet, after making love. Russell was no better at it than he'd ever been, but he did his best not to hurt her and to slow down before he came because she seemed to like that best. He had slowed down tonight, slowed almost to a stop, and withdrew nearly his full length, and as he was about to plunge in for the last hard thrust, something in his brain went black and he saw himself looking into a dark, deep pit and he heard himself say, "I'm gonna pour my soul into you," and at once he saw that if he went on, he would plunge into that pit, lost, without a soul of his own, and be damned forever. He thrust hard into her, and they came together, and it felt very good.

Now, as he lay in bed looking at the ceiling, he called back the image of this black pit, this pouring out of his soul, and he wondered what this vision could have meant, and what he had chosen, and what the consequence would be. He turned his head on the pillow and looked at Maria. Her eyes were closed, and he could see she was pretending to be asleep. She had hated him for a week, and then she had tried to love him, and now she loved him again. It was all too much for him. He closed his eyes and slept.

Maria noticed finally—and how had she missed it before this?—that sometime during the past month or two Russell had begun to love her the way she used to love him. She pushed the thought aside. It would be something to think about later. At the moment she had her high school graduation to think of, and her morning sickness—she was pregnant for real this time—and getting the beef braised just right for her daube de boeuf à la Marseilles. Her mother was coming to dinner tonight and she wanted to show off a little. She dropped another gob of butter in the pan and it sizzled up and turned brown. "Shit," she said, and her heart sank. The heat was too high. She put some chunks of beef into the pot, tentatively, as

if she feared they might bruise, and waited as—
miraculously—they began to brown. Her heart rose.
Cooking was easy.

Russell was so happy he couldn't stand to be with Bog
during lunch break, so he invented an errand—a trip
to the bank—and drove off without bothering to eat.
He was happy because of the way things had turned
out. Maria loved him, and he spent every waking minute thinking of her, and he spied on her. He did not
consider it spying. He just wanted to see her, to be
near her.

He decided he would drive, just once, past her
school, and if he saw her he would wave and keep on
going. He slowed down as he approached the school,
but he saw only a postman wheeling a huge sack of
mail up the front walk. Nobody else. He drove down
the block, then three blocks, and made a huge square
and came back once more. He wanted only a glimpse
of her. A tiny little look. A couple teachers were out
front now, smoking, and there was a black kid sitting
with his back against a tree, but nobody else. Russell
slowed to a crawl, and when the teachers turned to
look at him, he stepped on the gas and got out of
there. He would go back to work. His mouth was dry
and he was getting a terrific headache. He shouldn't
be doing this anyway. She'd hate it if she knew. But
he decided—his head pounding—he would circle one
more time, just in case. Nobody was there. He parked,
letting the motor idle. He was sweaty and frightened

and he wanted to see her. He wanted her to be with him, only him. If he let her out of his sight, she would go, the way his mother had gone, leaving him alone, with nobody, with nothing.

A bell rang, long and loud. At once all the doors were thrown open and kids began to come out, at first only a few and then crowds of them.

Sick, disgusted, Russell stepped on the gas and drove away. He didn't belong here. He didn't belong anywhere.

The cooking phase had not lasted very long, and once again they were at Ana Luisa's house for dinner and TV. Maria had begun to show, and she had filled out quite a lot, and this time it was clear she was pregnant. She and Russell sat on the couch holding hands, and from time to time he would look deep into her eyes and she would look back at him with a melting look that made Ana Luisa turn away in embarrassment. She was glad they were so happy, but she knew that love like this couldn't last. She waited until Maria got up to go to the bathroom.

"So, everything's fine again with you two?" Ana Luisa said.

Russell nodded. "Wonderful," he said.

"You're glad about the baby? A baby is nice."

"Wonderful."

"Of course you'll have to share Maria with the little one. A baby takes up a lot of time." She waited for him to say something. "I wonder, perhaps, if you love Maria too much."

Russell looked up at her, sharply.

"Just a little bit too much. *Tantito?*"

Maria came out of the bathroom then. She sat on the couch with her legs tucked under her and her shoulder against Russell's chest. He put his arm around her and they folded into one another easily, naturally, as if it would always be this way.

Maria was six months pregnant and desperate to get out of that damned trailer. She had decided she would not go to work until after the baby was born, and so she was alone all day with nothing to do except watch television and pace up and down the tiny living room. It was impossible, she said.

"Look!" She got up from the table, put her dish in the sink, and then lay down on the bed. She hadn't moved more than a foot in either direction. "I've got to get out of this tiny place," she said, "or I'll go out of my mind."

"It's our home," he said. "You used to like it."

"It's a trap," she said.

He tried to think.

He was already working overtime whenever he could, and he worked Saturdays at handyman jobs for people whose houses he had painted, and he would gladly work nights and Sundays if he could, but there still wasn't enough money. Where was he going to get the money? The doctor bills were covered, more or less, but his medical plan was shitty, and he had to get together all that extra money for the hospital and for shots and for God knows what, and how was he going to do it? And now she wanted to move.

"Okay, sure," he said, because she had to have whatever she needed. "But where?"

"I want to live with Mama."

"We can't live with Mama. There's no room. There's no privacy. Her place is not much bigger than this."

"Well, it doesn't have to be both of us." She let that sink in for a moment, and then she looked up at him from where she lay on the bed. "You know?"

He stood there, uncomprehending.

"I mean I could go myself. And just live there with Mama." She could see him beginning to understand. "There's more room there, and I wouldn't be trapped in one tiny trailer that wherever I move I'm still in the same place. I've got to move around. I can't live like this. I can't live in a trap like some animal." She paused, and then rushed on. "I'm not like you. I've got to have air. I've got to get out once in a while and see people and feel that I'm alive. It's too much, you can't ask this much of me, who do you think you are anyway?" He was just standing there, sunk into himself. He looked old and shriveled. "Listen," she said. "I've thought about this, Russell, and it's the right thing to do. I'll move in with Mama, and she can take care of me and everything, and you can come over nights to see me. It'll be just like it was, except that I won't be going crazy in this place. Okay? Okay?"

She got up from the bed and put her arms around him.

"It's for the baby," she said, whispering.

She kissed him on the neck. She had him now. He would do whatever she asked.

"Okay?" she said.

He pushed her away, hard, and she fell to the bed. He stood over her, white with anger, his whole body trembling with rage, and he shook his fist in her face. Still no words came. He turned from her and, swinging wildly, blind and speechless with frustration, he drove his fist into the wall. There was a crunching sound and a dull thunk as his fist went through the wood paneling and struck the metal shell of the trailer. He punched the wall again and again. When he turned back to her, his fist was bleeding, but the worst of his anger was gone. "The baby," he said. "It's always the god-damned baby. That's all it was right from the beginning. You don't care about me. It's just him. It's just that thing. It's just that little . . . nothing."

She huddled on the bed, silent.

"You haven't looked at me, you haven't paid attention to me once in the past six months. You've used me and let me wait on you and work overtime and scrape around for money, just so you could be alone with that . . . thing."

"That's not true," she said. "Russell? That's not fair."

"It *is* true. You never wanted me. You never cared about me."

She let him say it.

"It's been you and him all along. Just you and the baby. That's all you ever wanted."

"Russell," she said, looking at him.

"Come on," she said, "look at me."

"Sweetheart," she said.

He looked up at her finally. "Sweetheart," he said, and his voice was bitter, but he kept on looking at her.

She concentrated hard, looking. You are the only one, she thought, you are everything in the world to me.

She repeated these words to herself, waiting for them to take their place in her look, so that her eyes would shine and he would see she loved only him, and then he would be hers again.

You only, she thought, it's you only that I love.

But her attention wandered and she thought first of the baby and then of her mother's house, and suddenly she realized she had lost him.

For a brief moment, though, he had convinced himself that she loved him and only him, that everything would be all right, and so at least he wanted to be saved. He still had some hope left in him and she could work on that.

"We'll both go," she said. "Okay? We'll both go stay with Mama."

He hugged her hard, grateful, terrified. Would he ever have her to himself again?

Maria's life was good now. By the time she got up each morning, Russell had already left for work, so she didn't have to deal with him and his incessant need for attention. If Ana Luisa was still there, she would make Maria a breakfast of eggs and toast and raspberry jam. It was important, she said, that Maria keep her strength up and have something sweet with each meal. Maria ate whatever her mother cooked. She was always hungry. And it was nice to be waited on. If Ana Luisa had already left for work, Maria would make her own breakfast—toast and jam, some cookies or sweet rolls, whatever was around—and then for the rest of the morning she would watch the game shows on TV. In the afternoon she had the soaps and the great maternal satisfaction of lying on the couch and feeling the baby move inside her. Getting comfortable, she imagined. Sometimes giving a kick.

This was the real reason she had wanted to come back to her mother's house: to be alone and at peace with her baby. Sometimes she would lie for hours, softly caressing the mound of her belly, talking to the little boy inside. It was a mystical experience, and it lifted her high above the boredom and ugliness of ordinary life. The old saint stories she'd heard as a child came back to her now and she recognized something true in them. This is what Joan of Arc must have felt when she heard voices, or Saint Teresa when she levitated. The experience was beyond words, but it left Maria feeling holy, chosen. At these times she could forget she had ever married. There was no Russell, there was no life at all outside of her and the baby. For all her advanced ideas, she admitted to herself now that this was what she had always wanted.

In the evening, if Russell didn't have a night job, she would sit with him and her mother, watching TV. He drove her crazy, looking at her with that big moony face, expecting, *demanding* that she return his look, stupid, full of love. She was fed up with all that. She had the baby to think about, and she deliberately refused Russell's look, and to hell with him. That's why she liked having Ana Luisa there while they watched TV. It kept Russell in his place.

Sometimes Maria would glance at him while he was eating or getting her a drink or shuffling around the little house, and she would wonder what on earth had ever made her love him. His Anglo name? His blue eyes? They were a pale blue, a milky blue. She hated the sight of them, to tell the truth. They were like everything else about him, weak and needy. Only his name was any good, and it was hers now. Hers and her son's.

On nights when Russell didn't have a job and there was no TV worth watching, they would get in the car—Ana Luisa too—and go out for a drive and an ice cream. The summer was unusually hot, and it was nice to drive up over the mountains and out to the coast. Russell would deliberately park the car at places where they had made love—on promontories with the sea crashing below them, or up above sandy beaches—but Maria pretended not to recognize the places, and even when he leaned close to her or tried to put his hand on her leg, she'd give him no response. She'd just chatter on about game shows and money and buying a summer house on the beach. She could feel her mother's anger directed at her from the back seat and she could feel Russell's neediness and despair, but she was carrying a baby, she was about to give birth, and she couldn't worry herself about them. Why did everybody *want* something from her?

On the way back, they would always stop for ice cream, which was stupid, but it was something to do. And then, finally, they would go home. Maria continually surprised herself by her eagerness for home. When she was a kid, hanging around with Michelle Gross and Jennifer Benniger, she had never let them see where she lived. She went to Michelle's house or to Benni's, but she never invited them to hers. They were rich girls, with nice families, and they lived in big houses with clipped lawns in front and back, with bushes and flowers all around and lots of trees. The girls understood why they weren't invited to Maria's, and they didn't seem to mind. Back then, shy and ashamed, Maria knew how they'd see her house: a Mexican nightmare, a pile of cement blocks painted purple. The road out front was unpaved, with no sidewalks, and there were big old American cars—some just beat up, some completely abandoned—parked every which way up and down the street, in driveways, on front lawns. She had seen it that way herself. But now, married and with a baby due any minute, she saw it all differently. The place was messy, yes, but it was filled with life. The people were poor, but they knew who they were and they had values and family traditions that mattered. They weren't white-collar criminals like some people. They had no pretensions. And her house itself was warm and cozy. A perfect place for a baby to be born. Approaching it at night, seeing the living room light left burning, she felt a surge of warmth and love that included even Russell. She would touch him at these times, just a hand on his arm or even a little nudge, and she could see him shed his despair for a minute or two and be happy with her. But these moments were unimportant, really. What mattered was the baby. What mattered was the coming birth of John.

Russell woke her in the night. He leaned above her in the secret dark and said, "Listen to me."

"Listen," he said. "My father did this to me. He took my hand and held it in the fire. There was never any accident. He did it to me. He made up the story about a bunch of kids playing around a fire, and I told it to the nurse at the hospital, and I told it at school, but the truth was he did it himself. Maria?"

Silence.

"Did you hear me?"

The night was black. The room where they lay was black. They could have been alone in the world. They could have been at sea.

"Maria?"

"I don't want to hear this. Why are you doing this?"

"You've got to know me. You've got to know about me."

"I know you."

"You've got to love me."

Silence and darkness.

She put her hand up and touched his face. It was wet, with perspiration or with tears; she couldn't tell. She let her hand rest there for a minute.

"I love you," he whispered over and over.

She fell asleep, her open hand against his cheek.

"I love you. And I love the baby," he whispered. "I love you."

John was born with a halo of blond curls and eyes as pale and blue as Russell's own. Russell looked at the baby through the glass window, tapped at it, got his attention. The baby seemed to smile at him. Russell was relieved to find that he was very happy. He loved his son. He would be a good father.

Later he saw Maria with the baby, a fat little blond thing wriggling at her breast.

"John," Maria said, "because it sounds so American."

Russell smiled at her, and at the baby, and at her again, but she did not look up at him.

After a while, though, she did look up, but vaguely, distracted. She did not see Russell at all. He could have been anybody. Or nobody.

She had eyes only for the baby.

That night—late, late in the night—Russell stood before the bathroom mirror and drew a razor blade, hard, across his chest in a huge X, as if in this way he could cancel out his heart.

TWO

The birth, they told her, was an easy one. There had been a moment, just before the baby's head appeared, when Maria felt her whole body splitting open. She wanted to die, and she wanted the baby to die, and she wanted Russell to die. But in the next moment she was almost done, and with another push, and another, and a long thin shuddering intake of breath, she gave birth. The baby was big, with Russell's squarish face and pale blue eyes. There were wisps of yellow hair on his head. Even red and squalling, he was the most beautiful baby she had ever seen.

Later, when the nurse brought him to her and laid the baby against her breast, Maria said, "He's beautiful, isn't he." The nurse said nothing at first but then, embarrassed, she said, "He's a healthy baby, thank God." She paused for a moment. "And yes, he is beautiful." Later still, when Maria was leaving the hospital, the baby in her arms, the nurse said, "It's an Irish thing, you know. My mother always used to say that if you praise a baby's beauty, you invite the jealous gods to put a curse on him. I know it's silly, but I always think of her when I see a baby like yours, that looks too beautiful to live." The baby spit up then, and they laughed.

The baby's beauty was not what fascinated Maria; it was the firmness of his flesh, the shape of each tiny feature, and the recognition in the baby's eyes. She spent hours each day just gazing at him.

She spent hours, too, remembering her old, nearly forgotten life. Her silly high school ambitions, her friends who were never really friends at all, and her old determination to get away. From what? From this good, full life? She realized now that a woman could have no higher ambition than to be a mother. She was ashamed that she had always taken Ana Luisa for granted, had been so mean to her about her clothes, her hair, her little shrine. There was a lot to be said for the old-fashioned ways.

When she thought of Russell—big, dull, loving Russell—she wondered how it could be that at some point she'd stopped loving him and started to hate him. Why was that? she wondered. What had he wanted and why hadn't she been able to give it? He was such a good man.

She was glad all that was over.

They were husband and wife again, loving but not crazy in love, and they had this beautiful child, John. Who could ask for more?

. . . . .

The baby was a kind of miracle in Russell's life. A tiny thing, perfectly formed, with fat little fingers and toes, he was a miniature person in every way, a miniature Russell Whitaker, but flawless. Russell was mesmerized. Weeks passed, and John's eyes turned from pale blue to a deeper blue and then to brown. His yellow hair fell out and grew in black. He had Maria's nose, her chin, her large expressive eyes. Russell watched, and marveled, but he did not seem to understand the change that had taken place. John was Maria's child now, and Russell didn't know it.

Russell could not get over the wonder of the baby: John sleeping in his cot, John waking up happy and surprised, John breathing, John crying, John's sudden smile at the sight of his daddy. Sometimes in the night when Russell got out of bed to change John's diapers or to give him a bottle, he would finish up whatever he was doing and then kneel beside the crib with his head resting on the mattress so he could watch the baby sleep, his little belly rising and falling, his clean sweet breath on Russell's face. At these moments, time came to a stop, and there were just the two of them in this world, face to face, breathing each other's breath.

Russell had determined to be good, and he was good, and the baby made it easy. No more jealousy, no more fits of impotent rage. It no longer mattered that Maria had lost herself in the baby. Russell had lost himself in the baby too. They scarcely noticed one another.

The house next door to Ana Luisa's was up for rent. They needed the space for the baby, they were agreed on that, and so Russell got a Sunday job at PayLess, and they scraped together first-month and last-month rent, and a security deposit, and they moved in. The house was even smaller than Ana Luisa's and it needed all kinds of repairs, but it was their own and they could spread out in it and there was a little sleeping alcove for the baby. Russell left the outside the way it was, raggedy-ass stucco that had begun to crumble, but inside he painted the walls a dazzling white. He sanded the floors and stained them and sealed the stain with polyurethane. He hung wallpaper with teddy bears and rocking horses in the alcove they used as the baby's room. Anything for the baby. It was all for the baby.

Whenever Russell found himself thinking of Maria and how she had left him for the baby, he told himself this: nothing mattered except the baby.

John fussed only when he was hungry. He gurgled and cooed and let out shouts of joy, but he almost never cried. "What a beautiful baby," people said. "What a happy baby." He kicked his fat little legs and smiled.

Maria's milk was not sufficient for the baby, and her breasts were sore and red, so after a couple weeks the doctor suggested bottle feeding. Maria missed that feeling of deep peace and surrender that came with the first warm tug at her breast, but it was a relief not to feel she was being devoured each time the baby nursed. And it was nice not to worry about what she ate and drank. And not to have something clinging at her all the time, even when she wasn't in the mood. Bottle feeding was probably better for the baby anyhow. A perfectly balanced formula, better than mother's milk. Nor did she feel any less a mother because Russell got up in the night and gave the baby his bottle. This was just sharing. She had John, after all, every day from morning to night, day in, day out, Sundays and holidays included. Not that she didn't love him. She loved being a mother.

John was a year old and had begun to walk and talk a little, and in all this time Maria had not asked about the fiery scar on Russell's chest, nor had he offered an explanation, nor had they once made love.

Ana Luisa mentioned casually that Maria had put on weight, and Maria got very angry. "Have you ever had a baby?" Maria asked her. "This is what happens when you have a baby. I'll lose it later." But months went by and she continued to gain weight. She began wearing peasant blouses with lots of ruffles, and big skirts in bright colors, and distracting earrings, but there was no hiding the fact that she was getting fat. "Do you think I'm fat?" she asked Russell, in a way that told him to answer no, and when he smiled at her and said, "No, I think you're beautiful," she shrugged and said she would go on a diet.

She began to sleep late in the morning. She would get up when Russell left, change John's diaper, give him a bottle, and then go back to bed, taking the baby with her. She liked to lie beside him, rocking him a little, stroking his back, and when he fell asleep, she too would fall asleep. But after a while she'd just take him to bed with her and say, "You sleep now, *chiquillo,* while Mama takes a little nap."

Sometimes she did not get up until noon. Then she poked around the kitchen for a while, fixing a late breakfast for herself and heating up baby food for John, and after that they'd watch television and have a snack, and before she had a chance to get the place straightened up, the day was nearly gone. Ana Luisa would be home next door and might come over at any minute. Or Russell might show up early from work. Maria would begin to rush around the little house. She washed her face, combed her hair back and plaited it in a single braid, put a clean playsuit on the baby. She tried to look her best when Russell got home.

The house was a mess, but what could she do about it? They didn't have a washer and dryer, and she couldn't get to the laundromat until Ana Luisa took her on Friday afternoons, so it was no wonder the house always smelled sour. And it was too small. There was no place to put anything, the playpen stood in the middle of the living room, and there were toys everywhere. She couldn't be picking things up every hour of the day. She was exhausted. Why couldn't every-body just leave her alone?

John lay in his crib singing to himself. "Mommy, Daddy, Daddy, Mommy." He had a high sweet voice, and he sang the song over and over again. "Daddy, Mommy, Mommy, Daddy. Mommy, Daddy, Daddy, Mommy." Sometimes he would pause, as if he were thinking, and then he would sing four Grandmas to make up for leaving her out. "Grandma, Grandma, Grandma, Grandma." It was a song he made up to sing in the dark.

The next time she took John for a checkup, Maria asked the doctor for some pep pills. He looked at her and then at the baby, who had a diaper rash and needed a shampoo, and he shook his head.

"Look at this rash," he said suddenly. "Babies get a rash like this from sitting around in wet diapers. Buy some Vaseline and some baby powder. And use it, for God's sake. Take him out in the air. He's pale. He needs some sun. Does he cry a lot?"

Maria sat there, confused.

"Are you depressed?" he asked. "Is that what's going on?"

She nodded.

"Is it sex?" he asked. "Is your husband catting around?"

"No," she said.

"Well, it has to be something. Look, you're not

taking care of yourself." He leaned toward her, his elbows on his knees, sincere. "You ought to talk to somebody. You need some help. You want to see a therapist, I can set it up on your health plan. Five sessions. What do you say?"

She was back in school suddenly, being bullied. "I don't need help," she said. "There's nothing wrong with me except I'm tired. I'm exhausted, that's all."

He continued to look at her in that sincere way, but she wouldn't meet his eyes.

"What does your husband think?" he asked.

Her jaw tightened and her lips were a thin line.

Finally he sat back. "Lose some weight," he said. "You'll feel better," and he stood up to see her out.

"Thank you, Doctor," Maria said, blushing, and she thanked the nurse, and she thanked the little boy who held the door for her as she left the building. "Lose some weight. You'll feel better." She was still blushing when she reached the street.

In the bus on the way home Maria went over his words again and again, trying to understand what had happened to her. He'd said, practically, that she was an unfit mother. She was neglectful. She was lazy. "Look at that rash," he'd said. "Buy some Vaseline. Are you depressed? Is that what's going on?" She blushed as she recalled the sound of his voice, the annoyance, the exasperation. She held John closer to her breast. She shook her head. To hell with the doctor. She'd simply put him out of her mind. She'd forget every hateful word he'd said. But over and over again she heard him say, in that awful dismissive tone, "Lose some weight. You'll feel better." It was so unfair. She had been doing what everybody wanted, having the baby, giving up a career, sinking deeper and deeper into motherhood, and now all of a sudden everybody was at her. The doctor, the nurse, her mother, Russell. What did they want? Why couldn't they just leave her alone?

She began to notice women on the street. They were all fat, every one of them. Fatter than her. She'd never let herself look like that. She resolved that tomorrow—today!—she would go on a diet.

By now the bus had left the deep city and passed through the residential district and come out the other side. There were fewer trees on these streets, the houses were close together, and then suddenly there were no trees at all. She pulled the buzzer to get off at her stop.

The sun was still hot, and where the cement side-walk gave way to a dirt path along the side of the road, the heat seemed to come up at her from the earth itself. John was heavy in her arms. She wished now she had brought the stroller, but she hadn't wanted to bother getting it on and off buses. She was tired. She was dizzy. She wanted to cry because of the heat and the dirt and the memory of the doctor's voice. She hoisted John higher in her arms.

And as she turned into her street, she saw it as she had not seen it since high school—hot and dirty and hopeless. The tarmac was torn up and puddled with oil. Huge old American cars were parked every which way, abandoned in front yards and driveways. No trees. No flowers. Just shitty little houses, skinny dogs, shrunken lives.

She was able to get into the house and lock the door before the tears came. She put John in his crib and pulled the curtain around the alcove. Then she allowed herself a good cry—because she had thrown her life away and because she had a mean doctor and because she was fat.

Afterward, she gave John a bath. She rubbed baby oil on his inflamed skin, she powdered his diaper and his bum. She gave him kisses. She was a good mother.

When Russell got home, he was astonished that Maria ran to him, her arms out, and cried against his chest. She kissed him. She clung to him. And then she took him to bed.

Russell tapped at the screen door, leaning close to it so he could see through to the kitchen. "Hello-wo-wo," he called, and tapped again. He held a bouquet of daisies in his hand.

"Daddy," John said. He came across the floor, eager and unsteady, screaming in delight. He was wearing only diapers, and his face was dirty.

"Some flowers for a pretty lady," Russell called through the door. "Is there a pretty lady in the house?"

"Daddy," John said, and pounded the screen.

"Oh, for God's sake, what?" Maria said. She came to the door and lifted the latch. "Why are you being such an asshole? Is that supposed to be cute or something?"

Russell stood there, the flowers in his hand, as she went back to the counter and continued cutting up a head of lettuce. It was not even twenty-four hours since they had made love.

"What?" she said, furious.

He put the flowers in the sink and, very gently, pushed her hair back from her face.

"Don't touch me," she said, her teeth clenched. "I can't stand it. And stop looking at me like that."

He was thinking, What about last night? We made love just last night.

She looked back at him, thinking, What I hate about you most is those milky blue eyes.

Neither said anything.

"Daddy!" John said, tugging at his pant leg.

Russell turned from her finally and scooped his son into his arms and said, "What a big boy you are. You come on with Daddy and we'll wash your little face and then we'll see what's on the news." He carried John into the bathroom and in a moment there was the sound of water running and then John's shrieks of pleasure.

Maria leaned over the counter, her body shaking as she sobbed, soundlessly.

He had tried hard for nearly two years. They had made love once, and he thought she had come back to him. Like a fool he had said, "I love you," over and over all through the night, and she had never said a thing. She'd only fucked him like a demon, up on top of him, grinding away as if she was trying to get a whole year of fucking into one night, and it was fine by him, even though she scared him with her raw hunger and her craziness. And then the next day it was over, for good. She hated him again, and she let him know it. He was fed up. He was done trying. He was going to drink instead.

Maria knew what to expect because she had read the booklet and listened to the tape they gave her. She was in the first trimester and the abortion was by injection of hypertonic saline solution, a simple procedure to produce contractions that would begin slowly and increase in frequency until the fetus was finally expelled. Discomfort, but no real pain. It was as easy as they said. Before Maria left the clinic, they warned her about the dangers of infection and excessive bleeding.

They warned her, too, about the pro-life protesters who were picketing the clinic and about the TV cameras that were there to record the event. They did not warn her—because how could anybody know?—that for a few seconds that evening her look of fright as she left the clinic would appear on television screens everywhere in California. Which was how Ana Luisa learned of her daughter's abortion.

Ana Luisa lit a candle and knelt down before the living room shrine. Taking the two small stones from their place on the little altar, she clutched them to her breast—one stone for each of her own abortions—and she said a dozen Aves. She touched the shell, a pinkish-gray clam shell she'd picked up on the beach the day she learned that, because of the abortions, she could never bear children again. Then, feeling old and heavy with sin, she got up and blew out the candle and went next door to take care of Maria. She would make her some hot chicken broth. She would make her chicken *fajitas*. Life would go on.

John lay in the dark, afraid to sing his song, because if he sang it, they might scream at one another and bang on the table and break things, and they wouldn't love him anymore.

After work, Russell hung out with the paint crew at Antonio's Nut House or the Old Pro or Pablo's. When they'd had a few beers and left to return to their families, Russell would look around for a game of pool or for somebody to drink with. Almost at once he discovered you could always find somebody, providing you weren't choosy. The idea was merely to drink and keep drinking until you could go home and collapse.

He drank at first to get away from her. And then to keep from thinking of her. And then to keep from asking for her love. He hated her, and he drank some more, and found he loved her still.

Tonight he was drinking with Bog. They had gone to the Miramar Café for Polish sausage and fries, and now they were back at the Old Pro drinking beer. Bog had been stood up by his date.

Russell leaned back on his barstool, staring up. Pin-ups of naked women covered the entire ceiling—centerfolds from *Playboy* and *Penthouse* and *Oui,* and here and there eight-by-ten glossies of unidentified women. Local talent, most likely.

"Tits and ass, that's all it is, Bog," Russell said. In the past year he had learned the language of the Old Pro.

Bog shrugged and drank his beer.

"No matter how you slice it, it's just another piece of ass."

Bog looked at him.

"What?" Russell said.

"What's the matter with you?" Bog asked. "You are one angry sonofabitch."

"Because I say it's just another piece of ass, I'm angry?"

"It's your attitude. You've got an attitude."

"I've got the right attitude."

Bog shrugged and shook his head.

Russell went into the men's room to take a leak. Afterward, washing his hands, he caught sight of himself in the mirror and sneered. He had put on weight and his face was red and swollen. He looked like a middle-aged drunk. He looked like his father.

At once, before he could turn the thought over in his mind—his father? that bastard?—his fist shot out and struck the metal divider between the urinal and the sink. The metal crumpled and the brackets lifted from the tile. Plaster trickled to the floor.

Russell washed his hands again and dried them with a paper towel. His skinned knuckles had begun to bleed.

Back at the bar, he ordered another beer and, as an afterthought, one for Bog as well. He turned to him and said, "So, tell me about my attitude."

"The way I figure it," Bog said, "you get what you give. You send out enough bad karma, and it's gonna come back to you the same way. You send out good karma, ditto. You get me?"

"Good things happen to good people."

"Right."

"And bad things happen to bad people."

"You got it."

"That's really deep, Bog. That's really profound. So, bad things never happen to good people, and vice versa. Right?"

"That's not what I'm saying. I'm talking about karma here."

"So how come you got stood up tonight, Bogdonovitch?"

Bog thought about that for a minute. "Maybe it was all for the best," he said, and laughed suddenly. "My mother always used to say that. She'd pray for something, and if she got it, she'd say, 'My prayers were answered,' and if she didn't get it, she'd say, 'Maybe it was all for the best,' so either way, she'd win. I used to say to her, 'Why bother praying at all, you know what I mean?' And she'd get really tear-assed." He smiled, remembering.

"So what you're saying is, I'm right."

"Sheez," Bog said.

They had another beer, and then Russell said, "I've got to go," but he continued to sit there.

Bog took this as a sign. "Listen," he said. "I want to say something to you, Russ, and I want to say it nice. Because I like you. It's about your attitude. You've got a whole lot of very bad karma churning around inside you. It's like you just swallowed a hand grenade and it could go off at any minute." He pointed to the blood crusting on Russell's knuckles. "You could turn into a very violent dude."

Russell listened, and it was as if he were two people listening. He was aware of himself standing at the bar, a painter getting a little homespun philosophy from another painter, and he was aware of himself as the man with the hand grenade inside him, ready to go off. And he could choose. He chose to be the painter, and he kept on listening.

"You've got this nice wife and this kid. You drink too much. You should be home with your family. Go on. Go on home."

Russell clapped him on the shoulder.

"Okay?" Bog asked. "I just wanted to say it nice."

Russell threw a couple dollars on the bar, punched Bog on the arm, lightly, and went out to his car. Violent? He was as calm as could be.

He drove home carefully, because you could never

find a cop when you needed one, but as soon as you had a couple beers, there was a cop behind every freaking bush. He'd never been stopped even once.

He pulled the car up on the lawn in front of the little stucco house. There was a light on in the kitchen, and he could see the blue glow of the television, so Maria must still be up. Bog was right. He had a wife and a son, and he ought to be home with them. Maybe they could start over. Maybe she could love him after all—if not right now, maybe later.

He went around to the back and let himself in. Maria was seated at the kitchen table, a cigarette in her left hand, her right curled around a glass. It looked like scotch in the glass. He was going to walk over and sweep her into his arms and kiss her. Good karma. But she saw him looking at the glass, and before he could make a move toward her, she said, "It's tea. So don't get your hopes up."

He didn't say anything. He was not going to let her get to him. He walked through the kitchen to the little alcove and, stooping over the crib, he gathered his son into his arms and lifted him high into the air the way he used to when John was still a baby. But John was two and a half now, and he'd been deep asleep, and as his father lifted him into the air and then squeezed him to his chest, he screamed in fright.

"Put him down," Maria said, "put that baby down," and she pummeled Russell with her fists, shouting.

John screamed, and Maria began to cry, but Russell danced with him across the kitchen floor, saying,

"You're my little son, and we're doing our little dance. Shhh. Shhh," but the baby only screamed more loudly. Russell laughed and kept on singing. Finally he became aware of Maria punching him and the baby crying, and he stopped, confused. "Here," he said, and thrust the baby toward her. She took him and went into the bedroom, and Russell sat at the kitchen table, waiting.

After a long while, the crying stopped and he could hear only the sound of Maria singing a lullaby. Then the singing stopped and Maria stood before him.

"Are you out of your mind?" she said. "Has the booze made you lose your fucking mind?"

He bowed his head and said nothing.

"You make me sick," she said. "You make me want to throw up. I wish to God I'd never laid eyes on you. You've ruined my life, but no more. No more! By God, I'm getting out of this trap, and you're never going to see me again."

Still he said nothing.

"I detest you. I . . ."

He looked at her finally, and she stopped. His face was white, bloodless. He got up and walked over to her. He stood above her. He said, quietly, "I live here too, you know," and he moved to the back door. Quickly, before she could realize what was happening, he put his fist through the glass in the door, and then he swung around and put his fist through the wall next to it. "I live here too!" he shouted, a crazy man.

The baby woke and began to cry.

Russell punched the refrigerator and the stove, he beat the doorposts with his fists, he shouted.

Maria snatched up the baby and ran out the front door to her mother's house.

When the police came, they found the kitchen a shambles, but the husband, who had done all the damage, was sitting quietly at the table, his head bowed, his hands folded. "I'm sorry," he said. There was no mark on the woman or the child, and the police concluded that she had probably been cheating on him or something and he just lost it and broke some furniture. They couldn't arrest him for that. They gave the two of them a warning and went back to their car. Nothing unusual. Just more of the same.

Ana Luisa decided to take things into her own hands. On Friday afternoon, therefore, she and Maria drove up to the Stanford Shopping Mall. She had planned the trip carefully, she had paid for a baby-sitter, she had helped Maria with her hair. It was her treat, she said. She bought Maria a sweater and a wool skirt at Talbot's, some good black pumps at Nordstrom's, and then, to set the mood, she took Maria window-shopping in Neiman's, Macy's, Jaeger's. "All these wonderful things," she said, "and all you need is money." Then it was time for coffee and she led the way to Café Andrea.

The tables were tiny and the service was slow, but there was real silver and real linen and the women having coffee were rich and beautifully dressed. Maria wanted to leave.

"But, Mama," she said, whispering, "it's so expensive."

Ana Luisa continued to study the little menu.

"We don't belong here, Mama."

"Have some of this," Ana Luisa said. She pointed to "Tiramisù," handwritten in lavender ink. "This is the best."

Maria flushed. Her mother's voice was so loud.

The waitress came and took their orders, and after a long while she returned with their coffee. "The cake will just be another minute," she said, and disappeared, apparently for good.

Maria looked up. Nobody seemed to notice them. She took a sip of her coffee, which was very strong.

"This is nice," she said.

"*Sí*," Ana Luisa said. "Now, *querida,* we have to talk about the marriage."

"Not here," Maria said. "Not now."

Ana Luisa looked around. The table nearest them was empty. At the other tables women were talking quietly, intimately, about their own marriages, probably. For a girl who once had so much ambition, Maria was not sophisticated at all.

"When?" Ana Luisa asked.

"He's crazy," Maria said, and lowered her voice. "I don't want to talk about it. He's crazy and he's a drunk and I just want out."

"He's your husband," Ana Luisa said. "You can't

get out. You have to ignore him and go ahead by yourself. He'll follow. They always do."

"He drinks up all his money."

"Then get your own."

"Sure. Oh, sure. I'll rob a bank."

The waitress stood there with two squares of cake, creamy in the middle, a dusting of cocoa on top. "Tiramisù," she said, making it clear she had heard nothing. "And I'll bring more coffee."

Ana Luisa ignored the cake and leaned across the table. "Get a job," she said. "Lose some weight. You've got a child you're responsible for. You can't just sit around watching television all day and complaining about Russell all night. You've got to do something. You've got to get ahead. What ever happened to your old ambition? You've got to make something of yourself."

Maria lowered her head, and for a moment Ana Luisa thought she might be crying.

"Try this cake, *mi niña,*" she said. "It's very nice."

The waitress returned and filled their coffee cups again. "There," she said, hovering. "Is everything fine?" And when Ana Luisa nodded, she said, "Lovely," and went away, professionally oblivious.

"I can't do anything," Maria said finally. "I don't know how. I couldn't even be a waitress."

"You can type," Ana Luisa said. "You've got that nice typewriter I bought you for college."

"I can't even do that anymore."

"You can lose weight. Anybody can do that. And

when you lose some weight, maybe you'll remember how to type. You never know. Maybe you'll want to."

Maria smiled. Her mother was trying. "I'll lose weight," she said. "I promise."

"Good, good, *querida*. Good for you. Now eat some cake. It's very nice."

Maria put her fork into the cake. It was light and creamy, and when she tasted it, she discovered it was flavored with rum. It was like nothing she had ever eaten. She took another bite. So this is what it meant to be rich—to have coffee and cake on Friday afternoon and never even worry about gaining weight.

She would diet tomorrow. That was a promise.

John was dreaming again, the same dream he always had.

In this dream, he was very tired, but he couldn't let himself go to sleep because he had to keep the block from falling. It was a big square block—like his alphabet blocks, only bigger—and it was up at the ceiling, in the corner of his room. He had to keep looking at it, and then it wouldn't fall. But if he looked away, even for a second, it would begin to come down on him, and as it came down it got bigger and bigger, filling up the entire room, crushing him in his bed. But it didn't crush him. At the last minute, just before he died, he knew somehow—but how?—that he had one more chance, but only one, and then the block was back up at the ceiling, in the corner of the room, and he was staring at it, trying to keep it there by looking at it, because if he could keep it there, the fighting would not start and they would not scream at one another and everything would be all right. He stared at it, and stared, but he must have looked away for a moment because suddenly he was awake, huddling against the wall next to his bed, and he was cold and wet.

Out in the kitchen his father's voice got louder and louder, and he didn't know why, but he knew it was his fault.

For John's third birthday, Russell bought him the biggest toy he could find. It was a giraffe, with tan and orange fur and a satisfied smile that made Russell laugh out loud. It stood five feet tall.

Buying it was not easy. Russell had been fired for missing work too often, and then taken back part time, so when he asked for an advance against his paycheck, the boss had laughed and told him to go fuck a duck. But Russell had pleaded—it was his son's birthday, he'd work overtime for no pay at all—and the boss couldn't stand pleading, so he gave Russell the money just to get rid of him. After work Russell drove to San Francisco to get the giraffe.

By the time he got home, they had already finished dinner. As he walked past the kitchen window, he could hear Maria and Ana Luisa singing "Happy Birthday," and he paused at the back door and looked through the glass. They finished singing, and Maria set the cake—white, with *Happy Birthday* in blue—

on the table at John's place and tried to coax him into blowing out the three little candles. She puffed up her cheeks to show him how, but John was too excited and just kept clapping his hands in delight. Maria gave him a big kiss and then blew out the candles herself.

Russell flung the door open and held the giraffe in front of him. "Happy Birthday," he said, his voice high as he attempted giraffe talk, and then he came out from behind the toy to give his son a big hug. John had moved forward to pat the giraffe, but when he saw his father, he pulled back, shy suddenly, and as Russell came toward him, a look of fear crossed John's face and he ran and buried his head in Ana Luisa's lap.

"John," his mother said. "What's the matter with you? Don't you see the nice toy your daddy's brought you? Isn't that nice?" And to Russell she said, "We didn't expect you. Not this early. And not sober."

Russell was looking at his son, who would not look up.

"He's getting shy," Ana Luisa said, and smoothed his hair.

"Or somebody's telling him things," Russell said.

"God! Not on his birthday," Maria said. "Do you mind!"

"Why else should he be afraid of me?"

"I thought that's what you wanted. Everybody to be afraid of you."

Russell sat down and pulled the giraffe over to him.

"John?" he said. "John, I want you to come here."

"Go to your father, *poquito*," Ana Luisa said.

"Now, John," Russell said.

John raised his head from Ana Luisa's lap. He was confused, and he looked at his mother.

"Go ahead," she said.

He walked to his father and stood looking down at his shoes.

"No, look up," Russell said. "Okay. Now, are you my good boy? Have you been a good boy today?"

John nodded solemnly.

"Of course you have. You're a very good boy." Suddenly Russell saw that his son had changed. His curly blond hair was dark brown, and his eyes were dark too. He had become the image of Maria. Russell reached out to touch John's hair, and at once the boy drew back and his little arm shot up to ward off a blow. "No," Russell said. "I wasn't . . . I didn't . . . ," but he saw that any explanation was hopeless and he gathered the boy gently in his arms, pretending none of it had happened.

He said, broken, "Happy Birthday, son. Happy Birthday, John," as if he had lost him too.

Russell was consumed with love. For over a year he had told himself he hated her, he told himself she had turned his son against him, he told himself it was all her fault, it was all his own fault, it was nobody's fault. But one morning, hung over as usual, staring into a gallon can of paint, he saw the truth and accepted it. He loved her, and she did not love him.

He felt as if his tongue were on fire.

Maria had taken a two-week course in computer programming, and though she didn't meet the qualifications for a job with Ackerman, Holt, and Sawyer, she was hired anyway because they were desperate, Mr. Lang said. Mr. Lang was personal assistant to Mr. Sawyer and did all the hiring. The firm was doing record business in wills, divorces, and tax cases, and the flow of documents was literally overwhelming, Mr. Lang explained to her, so they had to have somebody, *any*body, who could at least *type*. Mr. Lang said this apologetically, as if Maria deserved to know. He added further that one of their clerks was on pregnancy leave and another one, a male, might just as well be, since he was out more often than he was in, and when he was in he spent most of the time in the men's room, so she could understand, Mr. Lang said, the bind they were in. *Well,* now, he said by way of conclusion.

Maria loved the work. She sat at the computer all day typing complicated documents that dissolved marriages, made and lost fortunes, struck compromises with the IRS. It was exciting to be in a busy office, and though all the other programmers seemed to hate their jobs, Maria loved hers. She had a desk and a computer in the central pool, but she worked principally for Mr. Foster, who was young and just out of law school and who would be cute if he lost some weight. Maria herself had lost a great deal. She had her figure back, and she had cut her hair. She was earning money. Soon she would be able to file for divorce.

On Friday she worked late and Mr. Foster asked her to join him for dinner. She hesitated. He was her boss, and she was a married woman.

But Russell, she knew, would be out somewhere, drinking. And her mother had already picked up John at day care. Why not go and have a good time?

"Yes," she said, and even though he was fat and boring, she enjoyed herself. The food was good, and the restaurant was nice, and she was a woman out on a date with a man who was going to be somebody. She began to see that everything was possible.

Russell showed up late for work and the crew had already left for the job, so he said to hell with it and went and had a beer. He had another beer, and then he thought he would go for a drive. He found himself in south San Jose, near his father's place, and so he drove by.

The street looked the same as always—no trees, no shrubs, just rusted-out cars baking in the sun—but the house looked different. The front yard had been cleaned up and there were new stairs, the raw wood still unpainted, leading up to the door. So the old bastard had gone in for home improvement. Russell parked the car and stood in front of the house, just looking.

"You don't live there," a voice said.

Russell turned around, startled, and saw a little girl, not much older than John, crouching in the shade of an abandoned car. In her lap she held a cat with a sunbonnet on its head. The cat seemed perfectly content.

"You don't live there," she said again. Her voice was high and thin, and she sounded angry.

"How do you know that?" he asked.

"Because Uncle Emory lives there," she said.

Uncle Emory? The old bastard had become Uncle Emory? "And what's your name?" Russell asked.

Immediately the screen door banged open and a woman stood there, her hand on her hip, a cigarette in her mouth. "Janelle," she said. "You get in here. I've told you not to talk to strangers. Now you get in."

Janelle went slowly up the stairs, the cat dangling from her arms.

"Her name's Janelle," the woman said, making a point, and then she closed the screen door and latched it.

Russell shrugged and turned back to his father's house. He rang the bell, but there was no answer, so he went around to the back and tried the door. No luck. He checked the little ledge above the bathroom window, and sure enough the key was there. The old man was always locking himself out.

Inside, the house smelled of coffee. Russell stood in the kitchen and looked around, half expecting to see his father slumped unconscious over the table, but the room was empty. A checkered oilcloth covered the table, and in the middle there was a little wire holder for paper napkins and a set of salt and pepper shakers in the form of owls. A cup and saucer, a plate, and a frying pan stood in the drainer, and some odd bits of silverware were soaking in a glass. The floor was clean. Russell found himself getting angry at all this domesticity. The shelf over the sink had been fixed, he noticed, and the cabinet doors were all shut. The sonofabitch. Who did he think he was kidding?

Russell walked slowly through the other rooms. The linoleum in the bathroom was new, but the living room and the front bedroom were the same. Only now they were tidy. His father's bed was made and on the table next to it was a little blue book, *One Day at a Time: My Life in Alcoholics Anonymous.* There were some AA pamphlets too, and Russell opened the one on top, called "Let Go and Let God." It began with what looked like a prayer. "God grant me the serenity to accept the things I cannot change, courage to change the things I can, and wisdom to know the difference." He tossed the pamphlet back on the table. And then something at the head of the bed caught his eye. The spread was turned back a little and something black and silver showed from beneath the pillow. He lifted the pillow a tiny bit and then, shocked, pressed it back in place, smoothing the spread tight across it. He began to blush. There were rosary beads there. He left the room at once.

He was dizzy and his head had begun to ache. He should get out of here. He stepped into the bathroom and ran some cold water. He pressed it to his face and then looked at himself in the mirror. His face was bloated and there were deep lines beneath his eyes. He was becoming his own father. He dried his face and tucked the towel back on the rack. He should get out of this place at once.

Nonetheless he stopped at the door of his old room and looked inside. It was even smaller than he remembered. There were new window shades, but everything else was the same. The little iron bed, the kitchen chair next to it, the battered oak dresser from Goodwill. It could be any boy's room, he thought, and smiled bitterly.

As he was getting into his car, he heard Janelle calling goodbye. She was standing by the screen door, the cat struggling in her arms. He stopped and waved to her. She waved back, and as she did, the cat broke free and dashed around the side of the house and was gone.

Janelle kept on waving.

He drove aimlessly and found himself across town, parked in front of his own decaying house. He stared at it, a square box somebody had faced with stucco that was crumbling now. He went inside and walked through the little rooms. None of it was familiar. Who were these people who lived here? He understood that they were Maria and John and himself. But who were they? In a dim way he recognized the furniture and the clothes in the closet and the pictures on the wall, but in another way, with a strange kind of clarity he could not explain, he saw that these were all foreign objects, they belonged to nobody, they simply didn't matter. He could burn this house down at any minute and not one living thing would be lost. Maria was at work. John was at day care. He stood, looking around, and he could almost hear the flames.

He sat at the kitchen table and slumped forward, his head on his arms. What was he doing here?

He went next door to Ana Luisa's house. They had lived with her while Maria was pregnant. He tried to remember those days, but what came to him was only a hollow ache, as if his insides had been scooped out. That's what he wanted, really, to have his insides scooped out—everything, his heart first, and then his stomach, and then whatever else was in there. He pushed his fist into his belly. If he could just tear himself open, he could spill the poison out.

He walked through the rooms, looking around. It was all meaningless, even the joke glasses hanging next to the mirror in Maria's bedroom. They were just a pair of glasses with big eyebrows and a nose attached. They meant nothing. In the living room, he stopped in front of Ana Luisa's shrine. His photograph was there now, and John's, both of them smiling. He picked up the seashell, turned it over in his hand, and tossed it back on the little altar. Meaningless, all of it.

He drove to the mobile home park and found the

trailer where they'd lived right after their marriage. Somebody else lived in it now. Diapers were hanging outside on a clothesline. He had put his fist through the wall there. Again he felt only that hollow ache.

He drove back to his father's place and looked at it from the car. Janelle was nowhere in sight. The house was closed and dead. And he was dead.

But he was not dead, and that was the problem. He drove north to Half Moon Bay and then south along Route 1 and parked finally on a cliff overlooking the Pacific. It was early afternoon and the sun dazzled on the water and the sky was clear and deep. He could not see or hear another human being.

He could walk to the edge of the cliff and take one step too many and it would be all over. Or he could start the car and ease it forward, slowly, until it dipped a little and then lurched, barely hanging on the edge, barely, barely, then—bang—hurtling down the side of the cliff, turning over and over in the air, landing with a hollow crash, half in, half out of the water. An accident, if they wanted to think so.

He watched the sun as it descended the sky. It touched the water and spread along the line of the horizon until all the world he could see was divided in two. Finally it was night. Still he sat there, looking.

Slowly, a smile came to his face. What was keeping him alive, he realized, was anger at that father of his, the hypocrisy, the lie.

And somewhere deep beneath the anger, hope. That

she would love him yet. That she would let him love her.

What John knew was that he had to be a good boy. But he was never sure what a good boy did. At nursery school he could play and run around and make noise, but when he got home, he had to be very quiet. His mother was studying. Or she was busy making the dinner. So he was quiet. Sometimes, though, she was in a good mood, and she didn't want him to be quiet. She would say, "What's the matter with you? Why do you just sit there as if you're scared to death?" But he could never be sure when she wanted him to be quiet and when she didn't. With his father, it was safer to be quiet all the time.

When he grew up, he was going to buy them a big, big castle on top of a cliff, like the castle in *Snow White,* and he would always be a good boy, and they'd be happy all the time.

Maria was given another promotion and another good raise. She had been with Ackerman, Holt, and Sawyer for over a year, and she'd been promoted every three months, so now she was studying nights to become a legal secretary.

Mr. Foster had asked her out again and again, but she always said no, even though he was an attorney. Foster was a loser, she could tell, and he was fat besides, so there was no point in investing time in him.

Time was money; she had learned that very quickly. And money was her ticket out and up.

She had plans for herself. These plans included money and a good job and a better house—and John, of course—but they did not include Russell. She couldn't look at him, with his milky blue eyes. She couldn't stand to think of him. He didn't come home most nights, and when he did, he slept on the couch in the living room. She almost never saw him, but it was bad enough just knowing he was there, and she always knew because he left money on the kitchen counter. A few dollars, nothing big. Just enough to infuriate her.

John was four now, old enough for preschool, and she didn't want him exposed to Russell's drinking and his violent moods, she told herself, and so she had the locks changed on the front and back doors. At the same time, she had Mr. Foster send Russell a registered letter saying that she was filing for divorce. The time had come. She had to get on with her own life.

Mr. Foster was glad to do this for her, free, but Maria insisted on paying him. From now on she'd owe nothing to anybody.

"You must be crazy! You must be out of your mind! Nobody in our family has ever been divorced."

Ana Luisa had been going on like this for half an hour, and Maria had stopped listening. She stubbed out her cigarette and waited. It was better to let her just keep raving until she stopped from exhaustion.

"You'll bring disgrace on our name," Ana Luisa said. "If we don't like our husbands, we ignore them or we scream at them or we hit them with a pan, but we don't divorce them. Never, never, never a divorce in our family!"

"Nonetheless," Maria said.

"Nonetheless! Nonetheless! What is that supposed to mean? Is that a reason? Is that an explanation?"

"Nonetheless, I've filed for divorce."

Ana Luisa stopped, finally, and stared at her daughter in silence. Maria stared back at her and lit another cigarette. She let the smoke seep about between her clenched teeth. Still Ana Luisa was staring at her.

"What?" Maria asked. "Say it!"

Ana Luisa blessed herself and said softly, "God will punish this. As you know." She turned and went out through the kitchen, where John was seated at the table making a mess of a peanut butter sandwich. *"Pobrecito,"* she said, and covered the top of his head with kisses, and then she was gone.

At home, she lit the candle and knelt down before the shrine. *"Virgen Santísima María,"* she said, "what a disgrace! That our family should come to this!" She sat back on her heels and bowed her head. If only she knew what to do. Her back hurt and her legs hurt and she had a headache, and what she really wanted was a nice glass of wine and the chance to lie down on the couch and watch *Wheel of Fortune* on TV. Nevertheless she continued to kneel before the shrine. *"Virgen Santísima,"* she said over and over, letting it go at that, since of course the Virgin knew all her troubles anyway. She ignored the pain in her back and legs. She gazed into the Virgin's painted face, and after a while she lost herself in the smell of the candle and the shimmer of the flame. *"Virgen Santísima María,"* she said, whispering.

Some time passed. A feeling of peace seemed to flow from the statue into her own heart, and then to overflow her heart and fill the entire room. *"María."* The candle guttered out, and still she knelt there.

It was dark outside when Ana Luisa finally rose from the little shrine and went to the kitchen to prepare *chiles rellenos.* When they were cooked, she would bring them over to Maria and John, and they would eat them, and life would go on as if there were never going to be a divorce. Then maybe there wouldn't be.

Ana Luisa sang to herself as she worked.

Maria got up in the night to use the bathroom and, when she checked on John, she discovered him lying with the covers off, hot and shivering. His chest was wet and his forehead felt like fire. She got a cold facecloth and placed it on his brow. He did not wake up.

Maria sat beside his bed, waiting. When the cloth was no longer cold, she replaced it with another and continued to sit there. John was not sleeping, but he was not conscious either. His arms twitched, and his head rolled from side to side on the damp pillow. Whenever she touched his brow, he shook her hand away. His whole body seemed to burn. "Daddy," he said once, or so it seemed to her. Toward dawn, the fever broke, and he fell into a calm, deep sleep. Maria continued to sit by his side.

John woke up hungry, eager to go to nursery school. He had no sign of fever, and there was nothing to indicate he had lain thrashing in his bed through much of the night. Maria saw him off with Ana Luisa, and then she called the office to say she was sick. Dizzy, exhausted, she went back to bed.

The next night, it was the same thing. The high fever, the limbs on fire, the twitching, convulsing little body. "Daddy," he said, this time quite clearly. Toward dawn the fever broke, and he slept.

Her child was sick, and Maria had no idea what to do about it. She took John to the doctor, who examined him thoroughly, listened to what she had to say, and then frowned and shook his head. He could find nothing organically wrong.

"These things sometimes happen," the doctor said, "and then they pass. He's a fine-looking little boy."

"I'm a good boy," John said.

"But what is it? What's the matter with him?"

The doctor gestured for the nurse to take John into the next room, and when they'd left, he sat thinking for a minute. "How are *you?*" he said. "You've lost a lot of weight. You look good." He smiled encouragingly, but when he heard she was getting a divorce, and why, his look changed to disapproval, and he said, "Divorce is hard on kids. Even very young kids."

"My husband's a drunk," she said. "Besides, he's deserted me. I have to get on with my own life."

"Yes, of course," the doctor said.

"He's violent. He put his fist through the wall. God knows what he might do."

"Has he ever struck you?"

"No," she said. "But he could. He might. You never know with him. He just goes crazy."

The doctor nodded.

"It's *my* life," she said.

"And your little boy's," he said. "John's."

Maria began to cry, quietly. "But what can I *do?*" she said. "I've done everything I can. John is afraid of him. And I can't stand him anymore. I can't even bear to look at him. It's like he's locked me in a trap, and I've got to get out. He won't let me breathe. I can't," she said, and she began to pound her knee with her fist. "I can't do it anymore. I can't. And I won't."

"No," the doctor said, "I can see that. You're doing the right thing. You're doing what you have to do."

She stopped crying then and wiped her eyes with a tissue. "My mascara," she said.

"You look fine," he said, and rang the buzzer for the nurse, who came in at once, leading John by the hand. He was holding a green lollipop.

"Green!" he said to his mother. And to the doctor, "Green is my favorite!"

"I wouldn't worry about those fevers," the doctor said. "He'll be fine in no time at all."

But the fevers continued every night, and Maria continued to watch by his bedside. She was sitting there, drifting in and out of sleep, on the night Russell came back.

It had been raining for days, and it would keep on raining, and the sound was very soothing. Maria dreamed she was in a boat. The sun beat down and the boat idled among the water lilies. It was very peaceful. She reached out, trailing her hand in the cool water. She could stay like this forever.

When the knock came, she turned it into the sound of oars tapping gently on the side of the boat. But the knock came again, and a third time, and Maria sat up, awake. She glanced in at John, who turned from side to side on the pillow, his brow glistening with sweat, and then she went to the door.

Russell was not drunk, she could tell that at once. He stood there in his blue poncho with water streaming down his face and said nothing. Was he in one of his crazy moods? She couldn't tell, but she was not afraid of him tonight.

"I'm sorry it's so late," he said.

"The baby's sick," she said, her finger to her lips. "So be very quiet. He's got a fever."

"Oh. I should have brought him something." He was whispering. "A panda or something."

"Do you want a beer?"

"No." He made a move toward a chair. "Okay, yes."

"Which? Yes or no?"

"Can I sit down?"

They were still whispering.

"Do you want something to eat? Some cheese?"

"I got the letter from the attorney. You're divorcing me."

"I've got to."

"I know." He nodded agreement. "I know you have to."

They were like old friends getting together after a long separation. As if all feeling had been suspended.

Outside, rain beat against the windows.

"No drought this year," she said.

"No. No painting either."

They laughed.

"I've always hated it, painting."

"I know."

The rain let up suddenly and in the new silence they could hear the clock ticking. The mood shifted.

"How are you?" he asked. "You look beautiful."

"I've lost weight."

"You look really nice."

"I'm getting the divorce, though."

"Yes."

"You aren't going to oppose it. You can't, you know."

"No, I know that."

"Well, what are you doing here? In the middle of the night and everything? Are you out of your mind?"

He looked at her. He could rape her if he wanted, they both knew that. He could fuck her on the kitchen floor. Or kill her.

They both knew what he could do, if he wanted.

"Don't get funny," she said.

He continued to look at her.

She looked back at him.

"I just wanted to see John. Once. Before the divorce."

"Come on," she said. "Don't wake him."

They stepped into the little alcove, where John lay in a tangle of sheets. His face was wet and he kicked out helplessly against the fever.

"Daddy," he said, a mumbled sound. And then very clearly, "Daddy."

"I'm here, John," Russell said, and placed his hand on the child's brow. He sat in the chair next to the bed. "I'm right here, son."

John stopped kicking and for a moment he lay still, as if the fever had passed.

"I'm here," Russell said.

Maria left the room and ran the water for tea. She put the kettle on the stove. She stood there, hugging herself for a moment, then she went and stood behind Russell. "You'll have to leave now," she said. "You're disturbing him."

"He's a little better now," Russell said. "He's not so hot now."

Maria looked at John, sleeping quietly. "He always falls asleep toward morning," she said. "You had nothing to do with it. You've got to go."

Russell stood, then bent over to kiss his son's forehead.

"Will you just *go!*" Maria said.

He looked at her, curious.

"Now!" she said.

"He's the only thing you've ever cared about," Russell said. "Isn't he."

Maria struck out at him, but he grabbed her by the wrist, and then the other wrist, and held them tight.

"Isn't he," he said.

She turned her face away.

"Isn't he?" he asked, squeezing tighter.

"Yes," she said.

A single tear ran down her cheek.

"God damn you," he said. "You're killing me."

"There's a man in there," Janelle said, but Emory Whitaker paid no attention to her until he saw the back door unlocked. He pushed it open tentatively, peeked into the kitchen, and then made his way on tiptoe through the little house. When he got to Russell's old room, he saw that there was no need for quiet. It was just his son. Russell lay, unconscious, on his bed.

Emory sat beside him for a moment, until he found the smell of old booze suffocating, and then he got up and opened the windows. Russell's skin was gray, and he looked half dead. When he woke up—*if* he woke up—he'd have a murderous hangover. Emory Whitaker knew about these things.

He went to his own room and got his copy of *One Day at a Time* and placed it on the chair beside Russell's bed. Then he went to the kitchen to make dinner. He still hadn't gotten the hang of eating regularly, but it was part of the program, so he did it. Swanson's Hungry Man dinner. Salisbury steak. Yummy.

On the second day, Emory came home and found Russell still asleep. The book and the AA pamphlets were on the floor, and there was a mess in the bathroom, so Russell must have gotten up and taken a shower or something. Emory stood and watched him breathe for a while. His son. Russell had grown into a big man, tall and broad. And screwed up, Emory thought.

He busied himself tidying the bathroom. He put out fresh towels and a new bar of oatmeal soap. He used Windex on the mirror. Then he went into the kitchen and made a pot of tea. He toasted some bread, and buttered it, and put everything on a tray. He placed the tray on the chair next to Russell's bed, so that he'd find it when he woke up.

The next day when Emory came home, Russell was sitting on his bed, wearing only his shorts. Emory was surprised to find him up, and surprised too at how powerful he looked.

Emory stood in the doorway, and they exchanged looks.

"Hello, son," Emory said.

Russell looked away from him.

"Feeling any better? I'll make you some tea and toast."

"So what's all this?" Russell asked. "Part of AA?"

"Would you like some juice? Tomato?"

"I don't want anything from you."

"I'll get the tea," Emory said.

"Get fucked," Russell said.

When he was washed and dressed, he went to the kitchen, where Emory had laid out toast and jam and a bowl of oranges. Emory was pouring tea into a mug that said *Have a Nice Day!*

"I'm having lasagna," Emory said. "It's frozen, but it's good."

Russell sat down and took a sip of tea. He made a face, then took another sip.

"I know. It's tough," Emory said. "Try to get some toast down, if you can. It's whole wheat. The sooner you get a little food in you, the better you'll feel. And there's some B_{12} here." He pushed a bottle of pills across the table. "You need rehydration and you need a vitamin supplement. I'll make you some—"

"Since when did you get to be Mother Teresa?" Russell stood up from the table. "What is all this Mary Poppins shit? You." He said it as if it were a dirty word. "You."

"It's all right. I'm only getting what I deserve." He poured Russell another cup of tea.

"Christ!" Russell said, and stood there speechless. A moment later he slammed the door to his room.

That weekend Russell stayed in his room with the door shut. The divorce agreement allowed him to see John for two days every other week, Saturday and Sunday, providing he remained sober, but now that he was sober he seemed unable to move. He lay in bed and looked at the ceiling. Sometimes he slept. After a while, he couldn't tell whether he was awake or sleeping. Lying there, he was a boy again, listening to his mother and father fight. He could hear their voices rise with anger and with drink. He could hear the shouts and accusations, the bitter laughter, taunting, and then a scream, the broken glass, the body slammed hard against the wall, the dull sound of blows, and crying. He could hear them even when he knew he was awake—and his mother gone more than twenty years now, and his father in AA. He turned over on his side and brought his knees up to his chest. The shouts and the crying would echo in this room forever.

It was a weekend like so many Russell had spent as a child.

On Monday when Emory got home from work, he found Russell's door still shut. He tapped lightly and listened for an answer. He tapped again, louder, and then eased the door open. Russell was lying on the bed fully clothed.

"We have to talk," Emory said. "I have to say something to you."

Russell looked at him.

"I'm in AA, as you know, and I've got my life back on track, and I'm going through the twelve steps." He sat down on the end of Russell's bed. "Okay?" he asked. "One of the things we have to do in AA is make amends for the damage we did while we were drinking. We have to admit it and we have to do something about it. Anybody we hurt, we have to apologize to. You know?"

Russell said nothing, but he looked as if he had stopped breathing.

"So, what I want to say, Russell, is this." Emory paused, placing his hand on Russell's ankle. "If I've ever done anything to hurt you, I apologize. Sincerely." He saw tears forming in his son's eyes. "I mean that," he said, and patted Russell's foot. Then he got up and left, closing the door behind him.

Russell felt the tears pricking at his eyes as he held up his ruined hand before his face. He turned it over in the light and examined the pink and hideous palm. He turned it palm-down and looked at it. He could see his father's face contorted with rage as he dragged him, struggling, to the stove and forced his hand into the flames. He could hear the flesh hiss, and he could smell it as the pain struck, sudden and hard, a hot knife in his brain. He could feel his heart melting away.

Russell lurched from the bed and collapsed against the chair. He lowered himself to the floor and knelt with his head bent over till it touched the carpet. He brought his elbows up and dug them deep into his stomach. And then he raised his head and turned his face to the ceiling and—with no sound, with no sound at all—emptied out his grief and rage in a long silent howl that echoed only in his brain, but echoed over and over and over again.

. . . . .

Ana Luisa parked her old junker in front of the house and looked around. It was a neighborhood like her own, only worse. A little girl was playing in the dirt at the curb.

"Is this where the Whitakers live?" she asked the girl.

"Uncle Emory lives there, and I live here," the girl said.

The screen door opened and the child's mother called, "Janelle? You come here now."

"What's your name?" Janelle asked.

"You'd better go in," Ana Luisa said. She got out of the car and approached the house.

The girl followed her. "Do you know what?" she said. "My kitty made peepee on my blanket, and now I can't keep her in the house. She doesn't mind, my mama says, but I think she does."

Ana Luisa rang the bell.

From next door the woman shouted, "Janelle!" in a different tone this time, and at once Janelle was down the stairs and pelting toward home. "I've told you and I've told you," the woman said, shaking the little girl, and then there was a wet slapping sound, and a howl of pain and indignation, and finally the sound of crying.

Ana Luisa rang the bell again and listened, but she could hear nothing inside. A battered mailbox shaped like a lantern hung next to the doorbell, and through the slot in the side she could see a letter. She glanced over at Janelle's house, as if they might be watching, and then she lifted the letter from the box. It was a phone bill addressed to Mr. Emory Whitaker. So this must be the house. She dropped the letter back in the box and knocked on the door. She knocked again, firmly. This time she heard noise inside, the sound of a chair falling over, somebody banging things around. She pressed the bell.

The door opened a crack. She could see a man's eye, milky blue, and a part of his unshaved face. He reeked of alcohol.

"What?" he said.

"I'm looking for Russell Whitaker," she said. "Are you his father?"

He leaned his head against the door, and it closed. She banged on the door.

"Mr. Whitaker," she said. "I've got to talk to you."

"Mr. Whitaker," she said, shouting.

He opened the door and looked at her. Then he turned and went into the kitchen, where she could see him trying to pick up an overturned chair. She stepped inside and glanced around her. The living room was dark because the shades were drawn, but it was neat and clean, as if nobody ever used it. She followed him into the kitchen, which was a mess. There were dirty dishes piled in the sink, and the counter was littered with soup cans and jam jars and packets of frozen food. There was a jumbo bag of potato chips and two large packages of Twinkies. On the table was a bottle of gin, more than half empty, and a glass that was full. Which explained everything.

Ana Luisa took in the kitchen sink and the counter and the table and then turned her attention to the man himself. He had managed to right the chair and now he stood behind it, clutching it for balance. He was small, pitifully thin, with a sunken chest and skinny arms. He was wearing only a soiled tee shirt and trousers. His bare feet were filthy.

"I'm looking for Russell," Ana Luisa said. "His son is sick."

He looked up at her, uncomprehending. "Do you want a drink?" he said, and with difficulty managed to get himself into the chair. He touched the bottle. "Drink?" he said.

"Russell's son is sick," she said, "and needs to see him. Is Russell here? Do you know where he is?"

He reached for his glass and tried to lift it, but he was shaking too much.

Ana Luisa took the glass from his hand and banged it on the table. "Never mind that now," she said. "Just tell me where he is."

"I'm sorry," he said, and tears rushed to his eyes. "I'm not supposed to drink." Suddenly he began to cry. He leaned forward on the table, his head on his arms, and sobbed.

Virgen Santísima, she said to herself, and to him she said, "Stop that crying and be a man. Are you a crazy?" She shook him by the shoulder, but it did no good. He kept on crying like an idiot. Finally she gave up.

She looked around the room and thought that maybe she should give this place a good cleaning.

Throw out the garbage, at least, and wash the dishes. Pour the gin down the toilet. Make him some coffee. She looked at him, slumped over the table, and thought: men. They're all the same. Whether they beat you or cry on your breast or push their thing in you all the way up to your lungs, they're all children, they're all selfish. To hell with them all.

She left the kitchen and the house and drove back to her own house where everything was nice and neat and where—no matter what else you could say about it—at least there were no men.

Russell lay on the grass, as nearly unconscious as he could get. He had drunk a pint bottle of Thunderbird and had taken three black beauties and at last he was beginning to feel numb. He was neither alive nor dead, just suspended, and he didn't have to think.

He had been living this way for a year now, sleeping in the park at night, panhandling by day, taking handouts wherever he could get them, just part of the San Francisco scene. He was not waiting for some reason to kill himself or to kill somebody else. He was just waiting.

He lay on the grass with his eyes closed, numb at last. He felt nothing. He was incapable of thought.

But then a little breeze came up and troubled the leaves above his head, and the sunlight made patterns of the leaves, and on his closed eyelids there slowly formed the image of Maria.

Maria smiling.

THE SHRINE AT ALTAMIRA

Maria sad.
Maria with John.
Maria in love.
Maria in love, but not in love with him.

John was five and a half, thin and nervous, but tough.
At school he could beat up any kid his age and some
who were older. At home, he was quiet and polite,
even shy. He took out the trash, he put away his toys,
he never used bad words. Mostly he watched television
or sat in his little alcove with the curtain pulled shut.
He liked to hide in there, turning the pages of his
picture books. He was no trouble at all, except very
rarely when he got angry. He had his father's temper.
But he was a good boy.

Maria placed a small sheaf of papers on Mr. Ackerman's desk, where they'd be ready for him in the
morning. She did the locking up—his office, her office,
the foyer—and took the elevator down to the main
lobby. She said good night to Mrs. Mehta, the cleaning
lady, and to Raoul, the custodian, who was seated at
the Information desk reading the *Wall Street Journal*.
As she crossed the lobby, she listened with satisfaction
to the click of her heels on the marble floor and the
dull echo that sprang up around her. It was the sound
of her new authority.

That week Maria had been made personal assistant
to Mr. Ackerman and, in a way, this promotion put
her in charge of all the clerical help in the office. Mr.

Lang, that fag, had made the mistake of giving Mr. Ackerman an ultimatum. "I simply cannot work with that woman a single minute longer. Either she goes or I go," he said. "You'll have to choose." And of course Mr. Ackerman chose Maria.

She loved her job, or rather she loved the sense of power that went with her job. She got to the office early, and she left late. There was always extra work to do, and even when she delegated it, she supervised anything that went to Mr. Ackerman under her name. She was invaluable, Ackerman told her, and she intended to stay that way.

She went to the parking lot and got into her car. She flipped on the radio and pulled out of the lot, heading east on Santa Cruz. She twirled the dial until she hit a station where they were playing Buddy Holly. Rock 'n' roll. She loved the old songs.

She did not notice the battered Chevy that followed her from the lot, turned east on Santa Cruz, and continued on past her house after she'd parked and gone in.

She swept John into her arms and gave him five kisses—one for each birthday—and a sixth for his coming birthday. She greeted her mother. She collapsed, gratefully, on the couch.

Outside the house and down the street, Russell parked his battered Chevy and prepared to wait.

He had spent more than a year in San Francisco, drunk and drugged, not caring. But for the past month he'd been back in San Jose, living with his father, spying on his former wife, waiting.

If she went out, he would know where. If somebody came to the house, he would know who. If there was another man in her life, he would kill him.

His teeth ached and his breath was sour, with love.

Ana Luisa stood at the stove and gave another poke to the chicken breasts she was frying. It was foolish and wasteful to cook chicken this way, but it was how Emory liked it, and it was his house and his chicken, so she fried it for him. She couldn't get out of the habit of trying to please men.

"Russell's back," she said. "Where has he been?"

"Seattle, he says." Emory sat at the kitchen table, sipping Diet Coke. "But who knows?"

"I saw his car pull out as I pulled in."

"It's not much of a car."

"He doesn't come see John. He doesn't come see his own son. John is going to be six soon."

Emory said nothing.

Ana Luisa lifted a chicken breast to see how it was doing and decided it was not brown enough yet. She shook her head. What was so special about fried chicken? At least when you baked a chicken, you didn't have to stand next to it for an hour, coaxing it along.

"Fried food is not good for you," she said.

"He never even talks to me," Emory said. "He looks at me as if I'm not there. Here."

"He misses his son. It's only natural. He misses Maria."

They were silent then, with their separate thoughts.

When the chicken was done, Ana Luisa put aside two breasts for Emory to eat later, and she served him the other two—the crispiest ones—with green beans and new potatoes and corn bread. She sat down and watched him eat. They were both silent.

Ana Luisa missed Russell. She could see him in John, in the shape of John's mouth and chin, in the way he spoke sometimes, in his shyness. And in John's sudden anger.

But she could see no resemblance between Russell and his father. Emory was small and sickly, a weak, gentle man who spoke very little and, when he did, spoke softly. He seemed to have no anger in him at all. He was one of those men you wanted to help, so she cooked for him once a month. And in the back of her mind she thought this might be a way to bring Russell back into the family. Maria had not remarried. John needed his father. And divorce was a terrible thing.

Emory finished his meal. "Go on," she said, and he went into the living room to watch television while Ana Luisa washed the dishes and put them away. She sponged the counter and wiped it clean. She polished the stove.

"I'm going now," she called, and let herself out the back way. As she was getting into her car, she looked up, and as always Emory was standing at the front door, staring after her. She waved, and he waved, and then she drove away.

She laughed to herself. This had to be the strangest relationship between a man and a woman in the history of the world.

"It's just to the zoo," Russell said. "I'll have him back by five, I promise."

"Where were you when he needed you? When he was sick, you were nowhere around." Maria balanced the phone against her shoulder while she lit a cigarette.

"That was a long time ago. That was years ago."

"Only two. Not even two."

"Well, I'm here now. I've turned over a new leaf." Russell waited for her answer and felt himself growing hard. He put his hand to his groin.

"I'll have to think about it."

"I'll be there at ten in the morning. Saturday."

Maria thought about it. John was six now and ought to have a father in his life. It wasn't natural for a boy to grow up with just a mother and a grandmother. He needed a man's influence. And after all, the court had said Russell could have visitation rights two weekends a month, so she really couldn't prevent it if he insisted. Still, Russell was so crazy, so unpredictable. He had disappeared for a year, almost two, offered no child support, nothing, and then all of a sudden he wanted to take his son to the zoo.

The truth was he'd never gotten over her, and she knew it. So she might as well let him see John. What harm in it?

When Russell came by on Saturday morning, they felt strange together, oddly formal and polite. John, too, was strange. He seemed afraid of his father and was distant, quiet. John got in the car with Russell as if he were being taken to the dentist.

Maria spent the day shopping. It was a beautiful September day, warm but with a cool breeze, and she should have been having a wonderful time, but she couldn't stop worrying about John. What if Russell had one of his angry fits? What if he didn't have John back on time? What if . . . ? She refused to let herself think this way. She bought a new dress, maroon paisley, and she window-shopped, and she dawdled over tea.

By four o'clock, though, she was home, waiting.

Russell was right on time. At five, he dropped John off in front of the house, waved to Maria, and kept on going. John was excited, for once, and happy. And so now was Maria.

Two weekends later, Russell showed up once again. And again the visit went off well. John seemed glad to be with his father, and Maria was glad to have a day free for herself. By late November his visits were a regular thing. Every second Saturday, John was his.

Ana Luisa knelt before her shrine and offered prayers of thanksgiving.

· · · · ·

Russell asked if he could have John overnight. They would stay in a motel. They would have two days at Great America, sort of an early Christmas present.

Maria said she would think about it, and then she said no.

But Russell had already told John his plan—providing your mother says okay—and John was at her constantly. "I want to go. Why can't I go? I never have any fun." And later: "Other kids go all the time. I never get to do anything. Everybody's been to Great America except me." And: "You don't even let me see my own father. I wish I was dead."

Finally Maria said yes, he could go.

On the Friday before the Great America trip, Russell waited in the parking lot until Maria left her office building. She was wearing a new black coat and carrying a new black briefcase, and there was a man by her side. He walked her to her car where they stood chatting for a while. They seemed to have trouble saying goodbye. He was short, with dark hair and gold-rimmed glasses, and he seemed to find everything funny. He waved his arms around, imitating somebody, and he thumped the hood of the car as he made some point, and they both began to laugh. Even from this distance Russell could hear their laughter, hard and brittle, exaggerated. The skinny little shit was coming on to her.

They stopped laughing, and he said something, and something else. She hesitated. After a moment she put her briefcase in the car, locked up, and, smiling, they walked off arm in arm.

Russell was stunned. He was falling from a scaffold and there was nothing beneath him except empty air. He tried to get out of his car, but he couldn't seem to manage it. The door wouldn't open at first, and then he couldn't get his feet on the ground. The pavement gave way beneath him. He turned his ankle. He half knelt at the open door until his head began to clear, and then he pulled himself up and looked around. Maria and her boyfriend had disappeared.

She had a boyfriend.

Perhaps a lover.

Russell couldn't get his breath. He couldn't see. He stood bent over, leaning on the car door until his vision cleared a little, and then he took off after them. At once pain shot from his ankle up into his stomach. He stopped for a moment and then hobbled over to the parking lot fence and rested against it. He could see them—Maria in her black coat, the little shit with his arm at her back—as they paused outside Riordan's, said no, said yes, and then went inside. Laughing.

Russell stood for a long while leaning against the fence, thinking. Perhaps they were only discussing business. Perhaps they were only having a drink. He saw Maria's dark hair against the pillow. She was smiling up at him. Laughing with him. What was she doing out with some other man? Perhaps he was touching her hand across the table. Perhaps their legs touched. Maria grinned and gave a dirty laugh, twisting her body beneath his, and Russell wanted to choke the life out of her, he wanted her dead. He put his hand to his chest and traced the rough X he had carved in his body. He should have slit his throat instead. He should have slit her throat.

When they came out of the restaurant, it was very dark. They walked back to the parking lot, talking, not laughing now, and Russell could see that the boy-friend had his hand lightly on her shoulder. Not an embrace, really. Just a proprietary gesture that was more than friendship. Perhaps they were not yet lov-ers. At her car, they paused for a minute, and then she held out her hand. The boyfriend took her hand, but then he leaned close to her, and Russell could not see exactly what was happening, but he seemed to be kissing her. They stood there, close together. They kissed. He was sure they kissed. So perhaps they were already lovers. She got into her car and the boyfriend stood nearby while she backed out and pulled away. He stood, looking after her car. Then, jaunty as hell, the boyfriend walked across the lot and got into his own car, a red Mustang, and roared out into the street.

Russell stood in the shadow of the building, not moving, not even breathing, and then with his back to the wall, he slid to a sitting position and rested his head on his knees.

He was cold and the night was cold and he contin-ued to sit there, knowing now what he would do unless something happened to stop him.

But nothing happened.

The next morning at ten, when he came by to pick up John, Russell had dark smudges beneath his eyes and his voice was sharp and broken. Maria looked at him closely. She was nervous about letting him take John overnight, and she still wasn't sure she could trust him, but his face was closed to her. She could see nothing there to worry about, no signs of his craziness or anger. Maybe he was just tired.

"I've got five dollars," John said. "Look!" He held up five ones.

Russell knelt down by his son and smoothed his hair. It was the same color as Maria's. "Are you all ready?" he said. "It's gonna be a very exciting two days. Did you bring your pajamas?"

John was shy suddenly and moved close to his father's chest. "You know what?" he said. "Grandma gave me five dollars and"—he whispered—"I'm gonna buy Mommy a present with it."

Russell hugged him close.

Maria watched and, for the moment, she felt reassured.

"There's pajamas in here," she said, "and a change of clothes, and a sweater for tonight. It gets chilly." She handed Russell a TWA flight bag. "And his toothbrush and stuff."

"Sure," he said. "Let's go, John-o."

"Russell." She put her hand on his arm. He turned and really looked at her for the first time this morning. Suddenly she felt empty inside. "Russell," she said again.

"I'll be careful."

"Please," she said, and to cover the pleading sound in her voice, she said brightly, "John, come kiss your mommy goodbye," and she gave him a loud smack. John squirmed away and ran on ahead. Russell smiled at her, and still she could see nothing in his face. At the car they waved goodbye.

They had been driving for only a short while when Russell pulled off 101 and took a number of rights and lefts and parked his car in front of a ratty motel just off El Camino.

John gazed out the window and said, disappointed, "Is this it?"

"Almost," Russell said. "We just have to stop here for a short while."

"Why?" John asked.

"We just have to. Now, you be a good boy and wait for me here while I go see the man inside. I'll be only a minute." Russell made sure the car doors were locked, and then he waved to the boy and walked across the gravel to the motel office.

Inside the office, the clerk watched Russell coming, but as soon as he opened the door and approached the desk, the clerk got busy shuffling papers. Russell knew the type. He was one of those old farts who like to play I've Got the Key.

Russell waited him out.

"All right now, what'll it be for you, young man?"

Russell asked for a room with twin beds.

The clerk leaned forward with enthusiasm. "I can

give you twins," he said, "or I can give you a double. You'll have to make up your own mind. A double will save you a couple bucks—two twenty-five, to be exact—and it's cozy if you're with the little woman. Of course, twins are better if you're used to sleeping alone and you want a good night's sleep, though personally I think it's a damned shame. I think a lot of the divorces in this country happen because people sleep in twin beds." He paused meaningfully. "But of course everybody's different."

"Twins," Russell said. "It's just me and my son."

"Been traveling all night? You'll have to sign right here."

Russell signed the book.

"So, you been traveling all night?"

"No. Well, for most of it, yes. We need a rest."

"Sure. Going to Mexico? The Baja?"

"No."

The clerk was about to hand over the key, but now he stopped, the key still dangling in his hand. "No?" he said.

"L.A.," Russell said. "To see relatives." He reached out and took the key.

"I been to the Baja last summer . . . for the fishing, you know. Abalone. I tell you, you've never seen some of the fish like they've got down there. Squid. Big fellows, but nice and tender, not like they have up here. And then there's the abalone, you know. You scrape them right off the rocks, eat them raw. Very sweet and delicate. Now there are several kinds of abalone, most people don't know that. You take your basic abalone . . ."

Russell turned and left the office, letting the door slam behind him. He found himself beginning to get angry, and he could not afford to get angry. He could not afford any emotion at all.

"Come on," he said to John, "and bring your bag."

John followed him to the motel room. "But what about Great America?" he asked. "Aren't we going?"

Russell sat down on the corner of the bed and drew John to him. "I said we're going, didn't I? Don't you trust me? Don't you trust your own father?"

John looked down, and his face began to get red.

"You're supposed to love your father. Don't you love your father? Hmm? Don't you love me?"

John nodded his head.

"Of course you do."

"And Mommy too," John said.

Russell stared into the boy's dark eyes, touched his forehead, his cheek, his chin. It was Maria's face.

"And she loves you," Russell said. "Mommy loves you more than anything in the world. More than me, even." He pressed the boy, hard, to his chest, and his body shook with the love he felt for Maria.

After that, he put aside all feeling, and though things went very slowly, they didn't seem to be going fast or slow; they seemed to be happening out of time. He was himself but not himself. It was as if he stood outside his body, calmly, uninvolved, and watched this other self give John the sleeping pills and put him to bed. "But it's still morning!" John said. And Russell listened as he heard himself say, "It's still morning, John, but we have to take a nap before we go." He sat beside the boy until the pills took effect, and then he went out to the car and got the gallon can of paint thinner he had put there hours earlier. He watched himself as he soaked the mattress with the thinner, getting it in close to the boy's body but careful not to wake him. John twitched as the cold fluid soaked into the mattress and spread beneath him, but he did not wake up.

Russell stood there waiting. He sat on the side of the bed and watched John sleeping. He moved over and sat on the other bed, giving someone time to come to the door and stop what was about to happen. He waited for the phone to ring, for an earthquake, for a lightning bolt. But nothing happened, and he watched himself waiting.

Finally he got up and went to the little desk. He had not brought matches. He was trying to leave this to chance. If there were no matches in the desk, he would wake John and they would go to Great America and ride the rides and then go home. But there was a matchbook in the desk, a single match inside. The cover said "Can you draw me?" above the silhouette of a pretty girl.

He had delayed long enough. He walked to the foot of the bed and took one last look at his sleeping son. John's leg twitched and he frowned a little.

At once Russell drew the match across the striking

pad and tossed it on the bed. There was a whooshing sound, and a sheet of fire leapt up, blue and then orange, and the boy was enveloped in flames.

Russell walked from the room and lay down on his face in the shade of the motel sign. The grass was cool against his cheek and he felt, finally, that it was time for him to sleep. Distantly he heard the hollow roar of the flames, the sound of feet running, screams, and then the fire engine and the ambulance and the hospital emergency crew.

His son's face rose before him, but it was Maria's face, full of love for him, and he closed his eyes and slept.

THREE

Houses burn down in the night. Teapots get knocked over. A child pulls a tablecloth and brings the scalding coffee down, or it's the saucepan on the stove, or the boiling water. A baby chews on a live electric cord. Cookout fires, charcoal lighter, a hot gas ring, pokers, candles, a single match left lying on the coffee table—and the baby burns. Sometimes it is not an accident. The mother burns the child. Or the father does.

The nurses at the Burn Center had seen all of this, and Peggy, who had been there longest, had seen even more. When John was brought in, Peggy looked at him and looked away involuntarily and then looked back. She had seen worse cases than John, but of course none of them had lived.

It might be better, she said to Dr. Clark, if John didn't live either. Dr. Clark said nothing. He was not God. He was just a doctor, and it was his job to do whatever he could. He began to assess the damage.

The mobile unit had given the child excellent care.

They'd reached the motel only minutes after the clerk's frantic call—"There's a kid on fire here!"—despite his inability to say where he was calling from. A quick survey of the body indicated second-degree burns on forty percent—chiefly the trunk, an arm, a hand, a leg—and full-thickness burns on perhaps twenty percent, with particular devastation to the face. The child, male, appeared to be five or six years old. They radioed this information to the Burn Center, where the on-line physician that afternoon happened to be Dr. Clark. Did these burns, Dr. Clark asked, seem compatible with life? There was silence on the line, and then a brief discussion, and the orderly replied that the child was breathing and in shock, or at least borderline shock, but the burns were extensive and most likely incompatible with life. Nonetheless Dr. Clark dispatched a team of paramedics to the site and gave instructions for basic life-support systems: oxygen and airway maintenance, fluid protocol, intravenous lines with Ringer's lactate to compensate for dehydration. They placed the body on a board, put compresses on the minor burns, and covered him with a sheet. Only the child's face remained exposed, though none of them could look at it. In twenty-seven minutes he was at the hospital and very near death.

In the emergency room, they were ready for him, more or less, and he was dragged back into life.

Dr. Clark checked the oxygen and the fluids. Mucosal burns of the mouth and pharynx had caused edema that could lead to blockage of the upper airways, so—gently and with some difficulty—he inserted a soft-cuffed endotracheal tube until the edema should subside. It was a risk, of course, but better than having to perform a tracheostomy later if the edema got worse. You could never be sure with burns to the mouth and nose. The nose was bad. Full-thickness skin destruction, burned cartilage: there'd be major deformity. And there was no skin on the forehead to let them reconstruct a nose, so they'd have to use the stomach or the underarm. That would come later, though, so he'd have to think about it later. Right now he had more immediate worries. He scraped the crusts from where the nostrils had been, and then he moved on to the ears. The ears were good. Only the helix was burned and, with luck, the cartilage might not be exposed and there might be no chondritis. With chondritis, the pain would be unendurable. The eyelids had swollen, but edema had not yet set in, and he was able to examine the cornea and eye for lesions. The cornea was hazy, but he could see the iris details, so he flushed the eye with saline solution and applied chloromycetin ointment. The prognosis for sight was fairly good, barring infection.

This was his job and he lost himself in it: saving what could be saved, repairing what could be repaired, cooling, cleaning, rescuing. He made sure he felt nothing.

He worked quickly and methodically, oblivious to everything except the job before him. Finally he straightened up and looked around at the rest of the team, three doctors, three nurses. They had been at work for more than three hours now, and the boy was still alive. It was a good sign. If they could keep him breathing, and keep infection out, he might yet make it.

When they left the emergency room, Peggy was thinking, The boy has no face, it's gone, it's melted. And to Dr. Clark, she whispered, "He won't live, will he." It was not a question.

"Fifty-fifty," the doctor said.

"It might be better if he didn't," she said.

"But we don't know what's better, do we," he said. "We're not God." And he thought, We're not so cruel as God.

They smiled a little and went off in their different directions, a doctor and a nurse, having done their job, or at least begun it.

John was playing on the beach, and the sun was very hot. It was so hot he didn't want to play anymore, and he asked his mother for a drink of water, but she only laughed and spread her arms and said, There's water everywhere, why don't you go swimming? He ran down the beach to where the wet sand began, but even the wet sand was hot, and the water kept pulling away from him until there was only sand, and the sun so hot, and nobody would give him a drink. He needed water, he thought he would burn up if he didn't have a drink of water, but then he remembered he couldn't have a drink of water because he had been a bad boy.

He couldn't remember how he'd been a bad boy. He promised he would never be bad again if only they would give him some water, just one gulp, one sip only. But they wouldn't give him water. And the sun was so hot. And the sun was so hot.

Dr. Clark lay in bed, unable to sleep, thinking of that boy. He would never have a child himself. They were too fragile, they broke, they burned. They died.

John, however, was not going to die. He was going to live, knock on wood, and so Dr. Clark forced himself to think ahead to the necessary operations: he'd need two to three surgeons for each one, Peggy and two other nurses to assist. And they'd have to be quick. The boy's condition would allow no more than three hours in the operating room at any one time, no more than eight to ten units loss of blood. It would take time, maybe years, to finish the job. And how many operations? A hundred? More?

At last he drifted into sleep.

He dreamed he was walking with Peggy in a strange city. There were no people in the street, no cars; there was not a sound. We shouldn't be here, he thought. He laughed softly, a nervous laugh, and Peggy turned to him and said, I know, but they kept on walking. Suddenly they heard crying and the screams of children. A fire, Peggy said, and pointed. He could see flames in the upper windows. The windows burst and flames poured out into the street, and there were children inside. Come on, he said, and together they ran to the building and up the stairs, but the stairs kept winding on and on, with no landing and no doors, so where were the children? They stopped. They could go on no longer. A door opened and a little girl stood there, on fire. He tore his coat off and wrapped her in it, smothering the flames, and then he ran down the endless stairs into the street. Then back again—he had no time to think of Peggy—and the stairs wound up and up and he couldn't go on, but of course he had to. Another little girl, her dress on fire. He put the fire out, then down the stairs and out into the street. Then up, another child, a little boy with no nose and no ears, then down, then up, then down, and so all night.

He woke, thinking of John. He would do what he could for him. He thanked God he had never had a child.

"Well, he's still alive," Peggy said.

"Knock on wood," Dr. Clark said.

"He must be terribly strong for such a little kid."

Dr. Clark said nothing.

Later Peggy said, "He must be a fighter. You can never tell who's a fighter just by looking at them. At least I can't."

And still later she said, "He is going to make it, don't you think?"

"I try not to think," Dr. Clark said.

. . . . .

Peggy had gathered the family for preliminary counseling. The social worker had warned her it was not going to be easy.

The mother was hysterical, blaming herself and cursing her husband, who—incredibly—had set the child on fire. She must not be allowed to see the boy just yet. The social worker was adamant on this point.

The grandmother was stoic. She spoke little English, but her attitude was hopeful and accepting, so she would be a big help when it came to family counseling, providing there was an interpreter at hand.

Peggy noted these things for future reference. No matter how brilliant the physician, no matter how successful the surgery, it was the family's support the patient depended on.

And John, with no face, would need all the support he could get.

On the third day, Dr. Clark decided John's left hand and arm and leg were ripe for grafting. They had sustained only second-degree burns, and the dead flesh could be cut away without much difficulty. He would do the hand immediately, the arm on the fourth day, the leg on the fifth. The third-degree burns on shoulders, neck, and face would have to wait until later.

To take the grafts Dr. Clark preferred the Brown dermatome because it was adjustable and it was fast, and what he needed now, quickly, were grafts of varying degrees of thinness. John's right thigh had been prepared as the donor site, and the lowest part had been lubricated with sterile mineral oil. After the first few cuts, the oil would not be necessary since the blood itself would lubricate both the skin and the instrument.

Dr. Clark nodded, ready to begin. The secret was to get tenseness of the skin from both ends of the donor site, and to work from the back of the thigh upward, so that blood wouldn't obscure his view and so the graft wouldn't fall in front of his advancing knife. He was an expert at his job. His assistant adjusted the skin tension while Dr. Clark pressed firmly on the dermatome. A thin, thin layer of skin rose from the boy's thigh in a perfect narrow strip. Dr. Clark laid it, raw side up, on a square of moist gauze and then returned to the thigh to excise another strip of skin. In less than an hour he was ready to begin the preliminary work for grafting.

To prepare the hand for the new tissue, he had opted for tangential excision of the old dead skin. This would allow him to remove the devitalized tissue slowly, layer after layer, until he reached a viable base, living flesh, where blood appeared. During the previous day, Peggy had applied an ointment to the wound every eight hours and by now the charred skin had been toughened and the wound was translucent. As the excision progressed, Dr. Clark would be able to judge the viability of the skin beneath his knife.

He located the central zone of coagulation and, using a Humby knife now, he bore down lightly on the devitalized tissue. It was like slicing corned beef, the blackened eschar curling through the knife, crumbling, the smell of smoke still there in the dead flesh. He removed another strip. And then another. He kept on pressing deeper into the dead tissue until at last he reached a good base of living flesh, and there was vigorous bleeding. Peggy applied warm moist packs, and then he cut again, deeper, taking enormous care not to injure nerves and tendons of the fingers. Now the grafting proper could begin.

He applied meshed split-thickness grafts, 12/1000 of an inch, stapling them into place to cut down on operating time. He cut a strip of graft twice the size of the index finger. He made transverse cuts, a few millimeters apart, around the periphery of the graft to about a quarter of the width of the strip. He placed the skin on the exposed finger so that the graft lay naturally against it, taking on its contours and irregularities, as if the skin were a glove. Then he moved on to the middle finger, and the next and the next. He left the thumb for last, and the scarcely burned palm. When he was done, he dressed all four fingers in a layer of wet wool, and then applied a layer of ribbon gauze, dry wool, a crepe bandage, and—at last—a plastic splint to keep the hand in correct position.

If everything went perfectly, the graft would adhere in four days or so, and Dr. Clark would remove the dressing and inspect the wound. With the splint off, he'd encourage John to move his hand a little, opening it, closing it, so that beneath the bandage the skin would regain flexibility and become his own again. In six months the mesh pattern on his skin would begin to fade, but it would always be there, a reminder.

And that was his hand, one percent of his body, not critically burned.

Now, with the help of the two other physicians and the three nurses, Dr. Clark could move on to the arm. Later they would do the leg. And then the shoulders, the neck, the face.

All that would take time, of course, and healing, and many separate operations.

At the preliminary hearing the judge remanded Russell to a week of psychiatric examination to determine his competency to stand trial. Like everybody else, the judge presumed he must be a lunatic to set fire to his own son. When the team of psychiatrists determined that Russell was sane, the judge only shook his head. He appointed a court lawyer for Russell's defense and ordered him to be held without bail until trial.

Privately, the judge was relieved. Crazy or not, he wanted the bastard to fry.

Peggy finished cleaning around the hole where John's nose had been and checked to see if his breathing was okay, and then she sat down beside his bed. It was late afternoon, the first time she'd been alone with him today.

"You're going to be all right," she said, leaning close and whispering. "I know it hurts, terribly, and you wish the pain would stop, but it *will* stop, and you'll feel better again. Not right now, but in a while. Okay? I want you to know that." She laid her hand on the sheet close to him and pressed down a little.

"I can't touch you, John, because it hurts too much, but I want you to know something. Whenever I press down on the bed like this—see?—it means I want to give you a hug, and this is the best I can do. I'm giving you a nice hug now. Can you feel that? And there's no pain with it. It's just very nice, because I love you and we all love you here. We all want to give you hugs."

She sat beside his bed for ten minutes, and then fifteen, pressing lightly on the sheet and letting up, each pressure a new hug. At five o'clock she left him and went off duty.

It was Friday, dance night, and she and her friend Rebecca were going up to the city for a nice dinner at Fisherman's Wharf.

Unlike Rebecca, Peggy never worried about her weight. She'd been overweight all her life and had always been able to get any man she wanted. She wanted one tonight.

After dinner at the Wharf, she and Rebecca were going to hit the discos and—who could tell?—she might get lucky and hook up with some sexy carpenter and they could hammer away at each other all night long. She was up for it. Cha-cha-cha. Rock 'n' roll.

. . . . .

Maria worked late whenever she could, even typing routine letters and documents she would ordinarily have passed on to one of the secretaries. Mr. Ackerman had offered her time off, at full pay, but she insisted that she wanted to work because it helped her to forget. Forget the horrible things, she explained, not forget her son.

John was on her mind, she said, every minute of every day. He was on the critical list, and he'd remain there until all the grafting was done, because with each graft there was new danger of infection. That's why almost nobody was allowed in to see him. She had seen him of course, for a minute, on the day after he was admitted. He looked terrible then, not like a human being at all, but the nurse had told her not to worry too much, they do miracles today, they'd give him back his face. So when she thought about him, she just concentrated on how he used to look and told herself he'd look like that again.

She thought about John all the time, she said, but that was not really true. Most of the time she thought about Russell. To go this far, to do this terrible thing to their son, he must have been crazy in love with her, he must have been in terrible pain. The newspapers said it was incomprehensible, and the television said so too, and her friends at work, but Maria understood at once. She possessed him finally. He loved her more than she loved him.

He loved her and she did not love him at all.

· · · · ·

The psychiatrists who examined Russell gave him a battery of written tests and then conducted personal interviews. The written tests were contradictory, indicating both huge reserves of rage and bitterness and, at the same time, a healthy adjustment to society and to life. The personal interviews were more rewarding. Face to face, Russell answered whatever was asked, simply but fully. His manner was not hostile or paranoid or psychotic. He accepted blame for what he had done, and he expected to be punished. All three psychiatrists agreed that he was clinically depressed, possibly an alcoholic, and most likely an abused child. They pronounced him sane and competent to stand trial.

John woke up and it was night again. He had been having that dream. He felt hot and wet and he tried to wipe his forehead, but his right hand was tied to the bedrail. They had kept him like this for a long time now: with his neck in a brace so that he couldn't move his head, and his left arm held straight out in a splint, and his right hand tied down. They were afraid he'd touch the sore parts, the nurse said, so they tied his good hand to the bed, loosely.

He wanted to blow his nose. He wanted to wipe his forehead.

He had been having that dream again, but he couldn't remember what it was. It scared him, and he woke up.

He was in a hospital with a lot of other sick people

and they had all been burned, some even worse than him. Peggy had told him that. She pressed on the bed to let him know she was hugging him, but he wished she would just hug him instead. He wanted to hug her. She was a nurse, and she was very nice, but he wanted his mommy and his grandma. And his daddy.

His hand and his arm were itchy, the burned ones, and his leg was itchy. His neck and face didn't hurt at all, even though that's where he was burned worse. He knew this from hearing the doctors and the nurses talking. Dr. Clark was the worst. He was the one who always came to see him before the operations. And then they'd wheel him into that room and tell him to breathe deeply and everything would go dark green, and sometimes dark brown, and then the dream would start. He didn't want to dream ever again. He wanted to stay awake and go to school every morning and run on the grass with all the kids.

Somebody was groaning somewhere. Or crying. Everybody here was a sick person. And he was sick too, with burns. "His father did it," they said. "Can you believe it?" But he knew his daddy didn't burn him. He knew he had been a bad boy. He loved his daddy. His mommy always said he should.

He was awake, and then he was falling asleep. He could tell he was about to dream, and he tried not to, but he was too tired and the dream began. There was a light brown square up at the top of the room and he had to keep it from falling, so he concentrated hard and moved it slowly slowly slowly across the wall, but then it started to crumble, and pieces were falling, and he wanted to wipe his forehead and it was so hot and he just wanted a drink of water and he wanted it all to stop. Now.

So it had stopped. It was over. He could just sleep now and not dream.

But up at the ceiling in the corner of the room there was a dark brown square and he had to keep it from falling. He kept staring at it. He had to concentrate.

The grafts were taking very well, all of them. The neck, of course, was the most difficult, because no matter how careful the grafting, no matter how perfectly fitted the neck collar, there was always the possibility of contracture. The limbs could be exercised, the fingers could be forced apart with splints, but the neck—with burns this bad—was a special problem. The chin just naturally seemed to affix itself to the chest.

Dr. Clark had seen contractures so extreme that, to separate the chin from the sternum, there was no other option but to make a horizontal incision on the neck, cutting nearly from ear to ear. This incision, a gentle slitting of the throat, released the scar tissue and opened a huge defect involving most of the front and sides of the neck. Split-thickness grafts could then be applied and the healing started all over again. In some cases the operation had to be repeated two and three times.

John's case was very bad, but the neck grafts were taking well nonetheless. Dr. Clark had not allowed him a pillow, since it might tip the head up and push the chin forward. Furthermore, he had insisted on a plastic splint, U-shaped to fit the neck and designed to force the head backward, stretching and exercising the grafted skin. The splint had to be adjusted each week to maintain pressure, and John would have to wear it for six months at least, maybe for a year, but these measures seemed to be working well. Dr. Clark hoped to get away without—he hated the term—having to slit the boy's throat again.

He stood beside John's bed and smiled at him.

"How ya doing, young fella?"

"Fine," John said, and his facial muscles twitched as if he might be trying to smile. He couldn't do it, of course, but he kept on trying.

Dr. Clark had spent a long day in the operating room, and he had lost an elderly burn patient who died right on the table, and now here was this little kid, in agony, trying to smile at him. It was too much. "You're a brave boy," he said, and turned away quickly, because he thought he might cry.

The shrink was right. He was losing his objectivity, his professional calm. He was identifying with the boy.

This was dangerous and could only end in one way.

Maria and Ana Luisa stood outside the door of John's room, waiting to see him. They were wearing the hospital gowns, masks, caps, and booties required for visiting a critically burned patient and they were listening to the nurse's last-minute instructions with great care. They wanted to do everything right.

"What you have to remember," Peggy said, "is that it might be a shock. His face has been damaged, badly, but Dr. Clark is doing everything humanly possible. And John'll improve a lot more. He really will. All right?" Her voice was pleading. "The thing is, he needs to see you."

"I understand," Maria said, a touch of exasperation in her voice. After all, John was her son. She would love him no matter what he looked like. "We won't be shocked. We won't show any emotion at all."

"Just be yourself," Peggy said. "He's such a sweet boy."

She opened the door, and Maria went in. Ana Luisa followed, slowly, and Peggy stepped in behind them.

"John?" Maria said, her voice low and warm. "It's me, Mommy. We've come to see you."

John tried to lean forward, but his head was immobilized by the huge collar he wore. "Mommy," he said, his voice raspy. "Mommy!" He sounded very glad. He tried to put out his right hand, but it was tied to the bedrail and he could only move it a few inches, his fingers jerking back and forth.

Maria took a step closer. She could not see his face, because his head was tipped back and he had no pillow. It would not be his old face, she knew, but it would be just as good. They did miracles today.

"Mommy?"

"It's me," she said. "I'm right here."

She stepped up close to the bed and looked at her son for the second time since the burning. His neck and shoulders had undergone massive reconstruction, his mouth had been restored, and his lips too. But his face was swollen from the operations, and the grafts were raw and scarred, and Dr. Clark had not yet begun to reconstruct the nose. She had been told all this, many times, but seeing him now, she realized that this thing was her son and he would always look like this. She took a step backward, turned as if to leave, and fell into the arms of Peggy, who half supported, half dragged her out of the room.

Ana Luisa never blinked. "*Poquito,*" she said, and leaned over John's bed. "You are so beautiful. You are such a good boy."

And John, who had not cried all this time, began to cry now, saying, "I want to go home. I want to go home."

"Hey, Firebug! Come over here. I want to tell you something. I want to tell you what they're gonna do to you."

Russell was still waiting to be sentenced, and the guy in the next cell—on trial for rape and murder—had just found out from the trustee who Russell was.

"They're gonna set you on fire, Bugsy."

No reaction from Russell.

"They're gonna fuck you up the ass, a pretty boy

like you, and then they're gonna set you on fire." He laughed, a low slow rumbling laugh of deep appreciation. "You'll be in your bunk, trying to stay awake so that they can't set you on fire, but they'll outwait you—you know?—and finally you'll fall asleep. You'll be dreaming away about some hot twat in a bikini or your old lady, and all of a sudden you'll wake up because you smell smoke, and you wonder what's burning . . . and it'll be you." He laughed again, happy. "How many of those guys you think are gonna want to put that fire out? Hmm, Firebug?"

Russell sat on his bunk, looking at his folded hands, listening.

"You never been to prison, so you don't know all the treats they got waiting for you, Bugsy. Do you want me to tell you about it? Hmm?"

Russell just listened. He knew he deserved everything they'd do to him, everything, and he would not resist. He'd let them punish him. He'd help them.

"Hey, punk. Hey, Firebug."

"What?"

"You want a match?" And he tossed a lighted match at Russell, just to keep him on his toes.

At the insistence of his psychiatrist, Dr. Clark took the evening off and, instead of studying the journals or making rounds, he decided to see a movie. He went to the Bijou where they showed old films and where tonight they were showing *True Grit*. He left after fifteen minutes because, on film at least, he couldn't stand the sight of blood.

"Guilty, of attempted murder," the jury foreman said.

The judge gave an angry speech about constraints of the law in California, the heinousness of this particular crime, the need for judicial reform. He sentenced Russell Whitaker to the maximum penalty for his crime, twelve years in prison, which meant that with good behavior Russell could be paroled in six. The judge shook his head, in despair of the law. "Next case," he said.

Outside the courtroom, the photographers shot Russell from every angle, but each picture was the same: a grimly handsome young man whose face seemed made of stone.

The neck and chin were always a problem, and despite their elaborate care, a contracture had developed. Dr. Clark had no choice but to perform another operation.

Carefully, concentrating hard, he drew the scalpel across John's throat from ear to ear, exposing a gap in the flesh that could now be given a new graft. They could begin again.

The operation took just under two hours. The neck would take six months to heal.

Every day there was another story in the paper and another batch of photographs. John at school. John at the beach. John with his mother and father—long ago, in the good times. What reporters wanted most was a photograph of John as he looked now, but so far Dr. Clark had prevented that.

This morning, when he finished the newspaper, Dr. Clark cut out the picture of John as he'd been on his sixth birthday, a handsome little boy, smiling shyly at the camera. He put it on his bureau where he could see it first thing each morning. He threw out the rest of the newspaper.

The next morning, however, he retrieved it from the recycling bin and cut out the picture of Russell Whitaker. He shoved it in under his handkerchiefs in the top bureau drawer where he'd never have to see it again. It was a kind of talisman. The face of evil smothered in a handkerchief.

The new prisoners, the fish, had to wear white for the first few days so the guards could identify them. The uniform was just a collarless shirt and loose drawstring pants, but it set them apart from everybody else and gave the old-timers a chance to check out the new meat.

"That's all you are," Nicoletti explained. "Meat."

Russell was in his second week on fish row, and Nicoletti had just proposed.

"Call me Nick," he said. "You want to hook up with me? I like my women big. And I don't care what you done."

Russell almost never spoke, and he did not speak now. He just looked at this man, another fish, who was in for three counts of murder. He was huge, with a belly that was solid and a head too large even for his big body. He looked like something in a circus. He was thirty, and this was his third jail term.

"Well, what do you say? No force. I'll keep the others off you—no niggers, no spics. I won't even *sell* you to anybody else. I'll get you drugs, smokes, magazines, the usual. And you'll be my kid."

"Your kid?" Russell said. They were nearly the same age.

"Right."

Russell didn't know whether to laugh or to punch him out or what. "I'm not gay," he said.

Nicoletti laughed. "You're not gay," he said, and shook his head in disbelief. "That's rich. That's funny. You're not gay. You're not *anything* in here. You're *inside,* man. You're just another piece of meat."

Russell looked away.

"That's all you are. Meat."

Maria went to work and came home late and cried. What had she done to bring this on her son? What could she do to change anything? She loved him, she wanted to see him, but she could only cry, and clutch her fists angrily to her breasts, and cry some more. She loved him. She loved him more than anyone in the world. Didn't that count for anything?

New prisoners were kept segregated on the top floor—fish row—while they went through orientation.

They learned the prison rules, saw the staff psychologist, found out what special programs were available for study and work. This was a modern prison, a model prison. At the end of three weeks, the fish would be moved down with the rest of the prisoners and assigned to a work detail.

On the night before the move downstairs, the guard handed Russell a sealed note and said, "It's from your friends in D Block." He watched as Russell read the note. It said only: "We're waiting for you."

The next morning Russell was sent to the laundry room to learn how to sort sheets. And, no surprise, he was assigned to a cell in D Block.

"My name is Emory and I'm an alcoholic. I've been in AA for over ten years now, but I've never gotten a cake because I always have a lapse, about once a year, and I go on a bender. It's six months since my last drink."

He paused for a moment and crammed his lips tight together, as if he found this very hard to do.

"You all know who I am, and who my son is, and what he did, so I suppose you can imagine why I go on a bender from time to time. They gave Russell twelve years in jail. People say that's not enough time for what he did to that little boy, and maybe it isn't, but I can tell you this. He's got to live with what he's done for the rest of his life. And I think to myself that I'm partly to blame for what happened too. Because the only example he had when he was growing up was mine. He saw me drunk and beating on his mother, and I probably beat on him too, though of course I would never really hurt an innocent child, and right from the start all he knew was drinking and fighting, so who is to blame? I take a lot of the blame on myself. I ask my higher power to forgive me every day, but I never thought I'd have to live with something like this. What I do is take it one day at a time, and I try to let go and let God. And I know that when I slip, I always got a place to come back to. Easy does it. Thank you very much."

It was midafternoon and Russell's cellmate, Boyle, was out in the yard at the weight pile and Russell was in his prison cell, alone. The cell was nine feet long and six feet wide, large by prison standards, and Russell was able to pace up and down if he felt like it. He didn't. He stood with his back to the wall, facing out.

Russell had been in D Block for almost a week and he had received two more notes. The first one said: "Don't lose any sleep waiting," and the second one said: "See you later." Harmless, apparently, but Russell got the point. He told himself that whatever punishment he got in jail was punishment he deserved, and so he had decided to put up no resistance, but the continual waiting had begun to wear him down. And in the past five days he'd learned from Boyle's example that if they decided to get him, there was no way he could protect himself. The cell doors were opened at seven o'clock for breakfast, and they were not locked again until ten at night. During those hours, anybody who felt like it could come into the cell. Or two of them. Or ten. There was a desk at the end of the tier and an armed guard behind it, but the desk was some hundred yards away, and the guards didn't care what happened anyway. They knew—everyone knew—that the gangs ran the prison. The guards just ran the prisoners. And even after lockup there was no way to keep a cell locked from the inside. There was always somebody with a key or, failing that, somebody who could pick a lock.

It was hot in the cell and Russell felt his eyes begin to close. He thought maybe he would lie down, but he didn't want to be taken by surprise, asleep, so he continued to stand against the back wall, between the toilet and the bunks, and he let his eyes close just a little, to rest them.

Suddenly, they were there.

One was standing with his back to the closed door, guarding it. The other—a big guy—swung around and advanced toward Russell. He stopped a couple feet away. "You're trapped between the shit pot and the bed, sucker. You're gonna do what I say."

Russell said nothing. He didn't move.

"First, you're gonna drop those pants and I'm gonna fuck you up the ass. Then you're gonna suck my cock. After that, I'll tell you what to do."

Russell's heart beat faster and faster. He stood there, paralyzed, unable even to think.

"Drop them."

The one watching the door said, "Come on, Nails. Fuck him, for Christ's sake."

Nails reached out and grabbed Russell's shirt and pulled him out from between the toilet and the bunks. He was taller than Russell and weighed at least twenty pounds more.

"Get on that bed," he said, "and bend over."

Involuntarily Russell's fist shot out and struck Nails in the chest, hard. He staggered backward, surprised by the blow. A second later, though, he charged, and caught Russell in the belly with his shoulder. Russell's head slammed back against the iron rail of the upper bunk. There was a dull thud and Russell slumped a little and tipped to the side, but then he righted himself and landed a blow to Nails's face, making blood gush from his nose. Nails tore at him now, kicking at his groin, his ribs, fighting like a crazy man. Russell fought back, dodging the blows, until he landed a lucky punch to the neck, and Nails's head snapped back and he slouched against the wall, his tee shirt red with blood. He struggled over to the door where his buddy waited, sneering at him, and then the two of them went away.

Russell lay on the bunk, trying to catch his breath. After a while he smiled to himself. He had resolved to accept whatever punishment they gave him, to help them punish him. What ever happened to that resolution? It hadn't lasted longer than the threat of rape. Was being raped any worse than setting fire to your own son? Russell thought about that. What did it matter if he was raped? Didn't he deserve it? Didn't he deserve to be passed around from jocker to jocker the way Boyle was? Like a piece of meat? That's all he was, really. A piece of meat, with malice. He waited.

In less than an hour Nails and his buddy were back. They stepped inside, and the buddy closed the door and locked it. Nails advanced on the bunk where Russell lay.

Russell sat up, Indian style.

Nails stood above him and said, "Take off those pants, roll over, and spread your ass." When Russell said nothing and just kept sitting there, Nails reached into his pocket and pulled out a knife. It was crudely made from a wooden coat hanger and a spoon handle, but it was sharp and would cut deep. He held it up where Russell could get a good look. Then instantly, before Russell could react, Nails slashed with the knife and Russell's pant leg was slit from his knee to his ankle. A line of blood appeared on the white skin.

"Take them off," he said. "Or do you want me to cut them off?"

They stared at each other for a second, and then, as Nails slashed with the knife, Russell's foot shot out and caught him on the forearm, sending the knife spinning across the cell. Nails dove at it, scooped it up, and turned, but by now Russell was off the bed and in a fighter's crouch, ready for him. Nails laughed, tossed the knife in the air, caught it, and made as if to lean against the wall. But instead, his left hand flew up and, as Russell swung to counter the blow, Nails's right hand, the hand with the knife, cut straight across

Russell's chest. His shirt fell loose and blood appeared and Russell pulled back, stumbling against the toilet bowl. Nails lunged at him, aiming at his belly, but Russell twisted away and the knife sank into the soft flesh of his side.

For a minute everything seemed to stop. Nails stayed bent over, still holding the knife in Russell's side, and Russell's arms flew up as if he were surrendering, and the guy at the door took a single step forward, and paused. All three of them stood like this, waiting.

Then Russell brought his fist down and punched Nails in the side of the head. With a short gasp of surprise, Nails pulled out the knife and, slowly, reluctantly, sank to the floor.

Russell crouched beside the toilet while the buddy dragged Nails from the cell. A minute later he came back and picked up Nails's knife. Before he left, he leaned over and whispered to Russell. "Now you're in trouble," he said. "Now you're really gonna get it."

Russell sank to the bed, unconscious.

When Boyle came in, he patched Russell up as best he could. He got out a bottle of iodine he kept hidden for his own emergencies and patted it on the wounds. Then he put little Band-Aids in a long row across Russell's chest and a couple bigger Band-Aids on the wound in his side. "You're not gonna make it," he said. "That chest wound keeps bleeding. You need stitches." Later he said, "Do you want me to get the guard? You need the prison hospital. Let me get the guard, before lockdown." And later he said, "They'll come for you, you know. Once the guard goes, there's only the night guard for four whole blocks. You'll be alone for eight hours." And much later, lying in the dark, he said, "What's that X on your chest? Did they do that to you in reform school? Did your father do it?" Russell said nothing, and Boyle said, "I suppose your father did it. Or your mother. It's a weird thing to do." A minute went by. "Listen, do you hear how quiet it is? It's never this quiet." Another minute went by. "When I came in, I was nineteen years old. Nineteen. I'd had sex with a girl once when I was fifteen, behind the school, and then I had my old lady when I was eighteen, and that was the only sex I ever had. My second day in here, I had it up the ass twenty times. They just beat me up and did it to me. After that I got a jocker to protect me. Sharkey. Sharkey's all right, except he trades me around. For cigarettes. I hate it. When I get out, I'm never gonna have sex again, period. You know?"

Russell started to get out of bed.

"What are you doing?" Boyle said. "You're gonna kill yourself."

"They're coming."

Russell stood by the bed, one hand clutched to his side, waiting.

There was a scratching sound at the door. Then the slow, heavy rubbing of metal on metal, the shuffle of feet, and the blinding glare of a flashlight in Russell's eyes. There were four of them, maybe five.

Nails held the flashlight to the side so that Russell could see who he was, and then he smashed it hard against the side of Russell's face. Russell's fist went out, and he crouched for the attack, but he was too late. A knee crunched into his chest, and fists caught him suddenly in the belly, the ribs, the kidneys. There were fists everywhere. He couldn't get his breath. Somebody had him by the hair and was banging his head against the concrete wall, and banging it, and banging it, and then he went unconscious.

They argued about who would be the one to turn him out. They figured he was a virgin, and so each of them wanted to go first, but Nails said, Let's be reasonable; it was my plan and I'm the one that knocked him out. So they let him go first. The others lined up and waited. They wanted Boyle to suck on them while Nails finished up with Russell, but Boyle seemed to have escaped during the fight. Typical woman, somebody said.

All four of them had Russell, and then Nails was ready to go again, and this time he was slower, deliberately taking his time, and while he fucked him he burned little holes in his back with a cigarette. The others had him a second time, and then they got a couple buddies, and they got a couple buddies too, and it went on—running a train on him—pretty much all night. By that time, Russell was bleeding from the rectum, and there was everybody's jism coming out of him, and shit, so they decided to leave him for the niggers or the spics. But it was too late, really, so they

took off for their cells. By this time Russell had cigarette burns on his back in the shape of a heart, a little
joke, and a burn on the sole of each foot.

After breakfast, Boyle called the guard, and a couple
hours later some hospital guys came with a stretcher
and took Russell away. On his body was a note that
Boyle hadn't dared remove. It said: "Get well soon."

Maria could not bring herself to step inside the hospital again. She sent John lots of Golden Books, and
she wrote him notes about how much she loved him
and how she wished she could see him, but she did
not go to the hospital. Ana Luisa went every week.

"He misses you," Ana Luisa said.

"Don't start, Mother. Just don't start."

"He wants to see you."

"I can't."

"You're his mother."

"I'm his mother, and he misses me and wants to
see me, but I can't bear the sight of him. It makes me
physically sick to look at him, do you understand that?
I can't bear to *look* at him! Now will you stop?"

"He loves you."

"I'll go mad. I swear to God I'll lose my mind."
She began to cry.

"*Querida.* Maria. It doesn't matter what he looks
like. He's your son. He's your child." She put her
arms around Maria. "I know how you feel. Don't you
think I know? It hurts you to see him suffer like that.
I know, Maria."

Maria shook herself free and reached for a tissue.

"He's been there more than a year, Maria. A whole year without his mother."

"I'll go see him, all right? I'll go. Not today, though. I need a little time. I need a little more time."

"*Querida*," Ana Luisa said, and stroked her daughter's hair. "It's hard for you, I know. It's hard."

Dr. Clark sat in the living room with the lights out. He had a scotch in his hand, and the television was turned on to some detective story with lots of hollering and shooting and car chases—harmless stuff, the usual. He wasn't looking at the screen; he just liked the background noise. It made him feel he was in the real world, without any of the trouble of being there. More and more, he felt he couldn't cope with reality. It overwhelmed him. It crippled him.

Only this afternoon his shrink had asked him, What is it you *really* fear, secretly, in your innermost heart? Dr. Clark had laughed. He wanted to say, I fear getting up in the morning. Hell, I fear *waking* up in the morning. I fear getting out of bed. I fear that on the way to work I'll see a teenage girl who's fat and angry and has no life ahead of her except rejection. I fear John's pain, because I can't do anything about it. I fear being alive. He wanted to say all this, but at the same time he wanted to say, What kind of crap have you been reading that you ask questions about my innermost secret heart? And in the end that's what he'd said.

There was a pause, and the shrink said, But I mean *really*.

Really, he wanted not to talk to people, not to see them, not to be responsible. Who was he to be responsible for the world's pain? Really, he wanted to be left alone. He wanted out.

He shook his glass a little, making the ice clink. He didn't drink scotch. He didn't even drink wine. He had no vices. And he was tired to death of it all.

Really, what he wanted was to find John's father and kill him. He had never said that before. He had never thought it before. But that's what he wanted. That's what he feared.

All this time he'd been blaming God, for his cruelty, his heartlessness. But it wasn't God who had done this to John. It was a man, with a man's face that somehow concealed the face of naked evil.

He got up and went into the bedroom and opened the bureau drawer. The picture of Russell Whitaker was scrunched up, but Dr. Clark smoothed it out and studied it under the lamp. This was not the face of a monster. Certainly it was not the face of the man who kept him awake at night and made his days almost unendurable. Whitaker had light brown hair, blond perhaps, a squarish face with a good jaw, and a nose that was a few millimeters too long. It should have given him a hawklike expression, but it didn't because the eyes caught your attention and held it. They were pale blue, or gray, and they appeared innocent of all experience, as if the person behind them had nothing to hide, nothing to be ashamed of. This was the face of a priest or a social worker, full of dumb goodness. It was not the face of a man who had set his own son on fire.

Dr. Clark knew people. He had connections. Nonetheless he made many, many phone calls before he learned that nobody would be allowed to see Russell Whitaker for at least two weeks. Whitaker was being detained, in privacy. It was a disciplinary matter, that's all they could say.

Dr. Clark waited two weeks and called again. He had to look at this man, this monster, with his own eyes.

Russell spent a day in the prison hospital until the internal bleeding stopped, and then, to keep him from causing more trouble, he was transferred to solitary confinement.

The cells in solitary were called strip cells, for two reasons. The cell was stripped bare and so was the prisoner, although—for humanitarian reasons—Russell was allowed to keep the bandage on his back where the cigarette burns had got infected. Except for the bandage, he would remain naked for the next two weeks. The sheets were taken away, and the mattress. That left either the bedspring or the cement floor for sleeping. There was no light, but there was an old paint can he could use for a toilet. The cell was four feet by five feet. In the morning a trustee brought him two slices of bread and a cup of coffee. In midafternoon, a thin soup. That was it: life-raft rations.

At first Russell was aware only of the pain. It was like a fire that spread from his rectum throughout his insides, making him shake uncontrollably. He was icy cold and yet the sweat sprang from his body. Inside, he was on fire.

Later, when the fever passed, he was aware only of John. "For you, for you," he muttered, even though he knew he could never make up for what he had done.

As the days went by—he measured them by the slices of bread—he became aware that he had lost a front tooth and there were cuts on his face and chest. He had earned it all. He deserved this and more. The next time, maybe they would kill him. "For you," he said.

He did not cry. He gave no sign that he felt anything—not pain, not guilt, and not repentance.

Toward the end he found he was most comfortable on his knees.

Maria parked her car on the bluff facing out toward the Pacific. From here she could see only the waves, stretching to the horizon. There was no land, no beach, only water and sky.

She tried to forget herself in work, but John was home from the hospital again, and how could she forget? There he was, everywhere, with that ruined face. He was nearly eight years old now, and very smart, and he knew she couldn't bear to look at him. The pain was too much. She could not pretend.

It began to rain, and in a short while she could see nothing at all. She sat there, looking at nothing.

Ana Luisa picked John up at his new school—a special school for blind and burned and handicapped children. It was his first day.

"How was it, *poquito?*" she asked. "Did you learn a lot today?"

"Freak City," John said. "Retards and freaks."

"Don't mock God's handiwork," she said, and made the sign of the cross.

"Not very handy, if you ask me," John said.

Ana Luisa said nothing. She loved him. She would forgive him anything. What had happened was the will of God.

"It's cool, Gram," he said, seeing she was upset. "It's *muy bueno.* I like the other kids."

"*Bueno,*" she said, and laid a hand on the side of his ruined face. "*Bueno,*" she said.

Dr. Clark sat at the table, waiting for Russell Whitaker to be brought in. He had never visited a prison before and he didn't know what to expect. In movies the prisoners sat behind little barred windows like tellers in a bank, and their families crowded around trying to slip them a gun or drugs or—in the comedies—a cake with a file in it. But this was just an ordinary room, empty except for the table and four chairs.

If this were his shrink's office and he was waiting
for his ride on the couch, he would get up, walk around
the room, look out the windows. But there were no
windows here, and the room did not invite walking
around; it was too much like a cell.

How deep inside the prison were they? he wondered. And what went on in there—in *here*—where
nobody could see what was happening and stop it?
He had trained at Harvard and he knew what power-
hungry men were like, so he could guess what went
on in a place like this, where the only power they had
was power over each other.

He refused to think of that now, however. He had
come to confirm something for himself: that the man
who set fire to John was no ordinary man; he was an
aberration of nature, somebody outside the scope of
human feeling. God's terrible mistake. Otherwise what
hope was there for any of us? He cleared his throat
and shifted in his chair.

Was there any hope?

In his breast pocket he carried the picture of Whitaker that he'd cut from the newspaper. And in his
wallet, the picture of John.

He was about to reach for the picture of Whitaker,
to search the eyes one more time, when he heard
footsteps coming, the loud click of a lock, and then
the door opened and Russell Whitaker came in, followed by the guard.

"Twenty minutes," the guard said as he closed the
door. He slouched against the wall with his hand rest-

ing lightly on his revolver, prepared to watch them.

Russell sat down opposite Dr. Clark. He had been out of the hole for three days now, but his eyes were still attuned to darkness, and he blinked against the light. He wore handcuffs and kept his hands in his lap. He stared down at the table.

Dr. Clark looked at him and then looked at the guard. "Are you going to stay?" he asked. The guard nodded his head. "I see," Dr. Clark said, and moved his chair so that his back was to the guard.

He leaned forward to say something, but he couldn't find the words. Whitaker was exhausted, he could see that. And in the recent past, perhaps in the last couple weeks, he had been beaten badly about the head; there were contusions, lacerations, dark swellings. He had very likely suffered a concussion. The eyes looked pained, with deep black smudges beneath them. A front tooth was missing. He needed something for the pain, and he needed rest.

This was the monster who had set his own son on fire?

Clinical, detached, Dr. Clark leaned back in his chair and studied him: the shape of the forehead, the cheekbones, the thrust and angle of the nose, the soft flesh of the lips, the square jaw. With such strong, clear features, it would be an easy face to reconstruct. It was a well-made face, nothing special, no evident sign of evil.

Five minutes had gone by and they had not spoken. Dr. Clark turned in his chair and glanced at the guard.

The guard stared back at him, but he stood up straight and began to shift from foot to foot.

"Listen," Dr. Clark said and, surprised by the sound of his voice in this strange room, he said no more. After a while Russell looked up at him, and Dr. Clark was astonished at the softness of those pale eyes, the look of innocence. Dr. Clark found himself blushing. "I'm your son's doctor," he said. "I'm a plastic surgeon."

Russell continued to look at him.

Dr. Clark turned to the guard once again. "Do you have to be here?" he asked. "Couldn't you get lost for just a couple minutes?"

The guard looked up at a corner of the ceiling.

They were silent again. Five more minutes passed. And another five. Finally the guard couldn't stand the silence any longer. "I'll be outside," he said, and left.

Again Dr. Clark leaned forward, searching Whitaker's face for some mark that set him apart from the rest of us. "Listen," he said. "I have to ask you something. I have to know."

Russell looked up at him.

"How could you do it?"

Russell said nothing.

"Why?" His voice echoed in the room.

"I don't know," Russell said.

"Did you hate him? Did you hate yourself? Was it insanity? Some eclipse of the brain? *How* could you do it?"

"I don't know."

"Your own son." He was whispering now.

"Yes."

Dr. Clark studied Whitaker's face as if, by an act of the will, he could see behind the eyes and find the secret there, the bad seed. But he saw only pain. He reached for his wallet and took out John's photograph that he'd clipped from the newspaper. A handsome little boy, smiling.

"Your son," he said. "Before you set him on fire."

Russell looked at the picture and said nothing. And as Dr. Clark continued to study him, a tear began in the corner of Russell's eye. It ran down his cheek, clung for a moment to his chin, and then fell to the table. He had not cried once since the terrible thing he had done. He had not cried in the mental ward, he had not cried during the trial, he had not cried when they beat him and cut him and raped him over and over in his cell. But he cried now, freely, at the photograph of his smiling son.

Dr. Clark got up and left the room. He had come to look upon the face of evil but had seen only an ordinary face, a man's face, and the man was shedding tears.

This Whitaker was not a monster after all. He was just another man.

And there was no hope for any of us.

They had begun reconstruction of the nose. Dr. Clark had chosen to raise a tube pedicle from the inner side of the good arm. That was quicker and easier, he felt, than using the chest or the abdomen, because the flap of skin could be applied directly to the face at the second stage. The challenge was to raise sufficient tissue to supply a lining for the nose, since cartilage and bone had been destroyed. Later he would use a bone graft to support the bridge, but that was months in the future. Right now he had to get the pedicle going, and it looked as if it would work just fine. The healing would take months, but at least they'd made a start.

John lay in bed, recovering from the operation. He'd become resigned to them. They were his life now, and besides, the worst part was over, Dr. Clark said.

Dr. Clark came to see him every day. John liked Dr. Clark. Peggy was John's favorite but Dr. Clark was next. And then the nice lady who read him his books.

He was very happy.

Bad news. There was not sufficient tissue on the arm pedicle to allow for a successful nose graft. They had to start over, this time working with the abdomen. It would take three weeks, maybe more, before the pedicle could be attached at one end of the wrist. Another three weeks before it could be separated from the abdomen and transferred to the nose, then two weeks more before the removal of sutures, and this schedule presupposed that each stage would be completely successful. Later they could worry about contractures of the nose and the cheek. Right now they had to start again to build a nose.

Dr. Clark gave no sign of his disappointment. He remained cheerful and positive in his attitude. If you weren't going to kill yourself, there was nothing else to do but get on with the business of living. Attitude, he had discovered, was everything.

The nose flap had taken sufficiently well, and now Dr. Clark was able to perform an iliac bone graft. It was a simple matter of taking a bit of bone from the right side of John's pelvis and grafting it to the glabella to form a support that would serve as the bridge of his nose. It was not a difficult operation, but it was tricky.

Afterward Dr. Clark went for a long walk.

Peggy—since it was Friday night—had a big dinner and then she hit the dance clubs with a cop she'd just met. He was the only cop in California who could dance, so he claimed, and he added, nervously, that he was fantastic in bed. "Fine, fine," Peggy said. "Just so long as you can dance."

John held the mirror to his face and examined his new nose. "It's nice," he said. "It's cool." He wiggled the mirror around to get a look at the nose in profile.

Dr. Clark had warned him not to expect too much, and John had tried not to, but he had expected more than this blob of muck where his face used to be. He looked like some horror movie. He looked like shit.

John knew that he would have lots of time to cry later, so right now he faked an eager look and a happy voice, and he smiled up at Dr. Clark. "Thank you," he said, and he shook the doctor's hand.

Dr. Clark looked pleased.

Ana Luisa had knocked three times, but still Emory did not come to the door. Maybe he was late getting home. She shifted the bag of groceries from one arm to the other and waited for a minute, then she knocked again. There wasn't a sound from inside. Either he was not home or he was not conscious.

As she stood there deciding what to do next, she heard loud rock music, and then a car came hurtling down the street, a low rider painted with green and silver stripes. The music got louder and louder. The driver stepped hard on the brakes and the car screeched to a halt, the rear end bouncing up and down on its extra springs. As Ana Luisa watched, fascinated, the door flew open and a girl got out. It was Janelle. She was laughing, and the kids inside were calling out to her, but Ana Luisa could hear nothing except the crash of the music. In the next second the car took off, spewing dirt and gravel, and the music trailed it down the street. Janelle stood looking after the car, waving.

She was a pretty little thing, almost a teenager, and she wore a short black skirt and a tee shirt that showed her breasts to advantage. It hung loosely off one shoulder. She gave Ana Luisa a cold, hard look.

"Is he home?" Ana Luisa called.

Janelle smiled, recognizing her at last. "I can't see without my glasses," she said. "How ya doing, Ana?"

"I'm cool," Ana Luisa said, and they both laughed. John always laughed, too, when she said she was cool. "Is he at home?"

"Use the key, why don't you. It's in the back," Janelle said, and started up the stairs. At once the screen door opened and her mother was there, hand on hip. "Where the hell have you been?" she said. "Do you know what time it is?" and Janelle, her voice ugly, said, "Don't start with me, you. Just don't start with me." The screen door slammed shut and they continued to quarrel.

"Families," Ana Luisa said. She went down the steps and around the back and let herself in.

She had the *albóndigas* made and in the oven before Emory got home. When she opened the door to him, she could tell at once that he'd been drinking. His eyes were hooded and he had a crooked smile and he reeked of old beer. She didn't know what to say.

"I've got *albóndigas,*" she said, "my specialty."

He blinked for a moment and looked around. His crooked smile became apologetic. "I've had a drink," he said. "Just a beer."

She looked at him.

"A few beers," he said. "I had more than one. I had a few."

"Come sit down," she said. She had never seen him like this, except that first time, and of course she didn't know him then. Should she call somebody? What

170

should she do? When her Paco got drunk, God rest his soul, she used to ignore him or, if he got too friendly when she wasn't in the mood, she'd just push him off or hit him with a pan. But this man, who was in AA? What would you do with him? "Five minutes," she said, "I'll have it on the table. With a green salad and some nice corn bread."

Emory sat down at the table, shakily, and watched her as she moved from the stove to the sink and back again. "I suppose you're shocked that I've had a beer," he said. "A few beers. I suppose you think I shouldn't."

"I'm not shocked," she said.

"I suppose you think I don't have any reason to drink."

She said nothing.

"Oh God," he said, slumping forward. "I live a good life. I try and I try and I try. But I've got a son who sets his own kid on fire, a maniac, a devil from hell. And what am I supposed to do? I shouldn't have a drink?"

"Sit up," she said. "For God's sake, act the man."

He shot a quick look at her and then slumped back over the table. "What do you know about it, for Christ's sake. Chiquita Banana cooks me a spic treat and she thinks she runs the place." He stood up, pushing back the chair so that it nearly toppled over. "I run this place. I'm the master of the house around here. Just get that straight. Don't have any doubts about that." He stomped off to the bathroom.

He left the door open behind him and peed noisily into the center of the toilet bowl. "Hear that?" he shouted. "I run this place and don't you forget it." He flushed the toilet and slammed down the seat and sat on it. He had to get his bearings.

After a while he closed the door and knelt down and reached deep into the narrow cupboard next to the bathtub. He felt around blindly until his finger slipped through the knothole at the back. He pulled the loose board forward and grabbed the quart of bourbon he kept on hand there, just in case. He sat on the floor and took a long slug straight from the bottle.

"It's ready," Ana Luisa called. "It's dinner."

He smiled down at the bottle. Fuck dinner. A fucking woman telling him what to do. Keeping him from having a drink. He tipped the bottle up to his mouth again and drank. He was halfway there, he could feel it. In a while nothing would matter, and he'd lie down with his bottle by his side and stay drunk as long as he could. Drunk and peaceful. Drunk and happy.

Ana Luisa knocked at the door, sharply. "Your dinner's getting cold," she said, and went back to the kitchen.

He tried to get up, but he fell back and banged his head. He took another drink and then rolled sideways, so that he ended up on all fours. Bracing himself against the toilet, he stood up and waited for his head to clear. He could hear her in the kitchen, the bitch, banging pots around. Act like a man? He pulled the bathroom door open and lurched down the hall and into the kitchen.

"What the fuck is this?" he said.

She was at the sink, and she turned now and faced him. "*Albóndigas,*" she said. "Like a big meatball, with rice in it; very tasty."

He moved to the table and looked down at the mess she'd prepared. Spic meatballs. Did she think he was a fucking wetback?

He looked at her, and she was looking at him. "Act like a man?" he said. "You want me to act like a man?"

He grabbed the corner of the oilcloth and gave it a yank, hard. The dishes went flying into the air, there was a crashing sound, and he stood holding the oil-cloth in his hand as plates and bowls smashed against the floor and the *albóndigas* bounced off into a corner and the salad bowl rolled in a large circle and then a small one and then, finally, stopped. There was brown gravy everywhere.

Suddenly he was at her. He grabbed her by the wrist and yanked her forward and then back, so that she lost balance. He held her wrist hard with one hand while, with the other, he turned the gas jet to high. And then he bent her arm backward, twisting her hand toward the fire.

Ana Luisa saw what was happening and did nothing to stop it until she felt the flames on her hand. Then she came alive and pulled away from the fire, dragging him with her, and leaning far back, she landed a hard blow to the side of his head. His face went blank, and he looked confused, and fell backward against the refrigerator door.

"What?" he said.

She pinned him against the refrigerator, leaning hard against him, with her hand at his throat. "You did it to him, didn't you?" she said. "You burned his hand."

"What are you talking about?" he asked, reasonable now. "You've got it wrong," he said. "You've got it all wrong."

"Russell's hand. Your son's hand."

"He was playing around a fire with a bunch of kids," he said patiently, his voice dreamy, as if he were reciting from memory. "He threw some lighter fluid in the flames, and it exploded. That's all that happened. Everybody knows that's what happened."

She leaned closer and whispered to him. "I could kill you," she said. "I'm strong enough."

He smiled at her, lost now. "It was just a game," he said. "They were kids, playing a game."

She let him go then. She stepped back from him, got her purse from the counter, and left the house by the front door. She got in her car and drove, and she did not cry until she reached home and knelt before her living room shrine. When she was done crying, she said to the Virgin, "I should have killed him. And you know it too." Then she poured herself a glass of wine and tried to resign herself to the holy will of God.

. . . . .

John put down his book and closed his eyes to think about it. He was reading *Saints for Our Times,* and he had just finished Joan of Arc, and he was not sure how much of it he could believe. He believed she heard the voices, because they made sense and because she was a saint and everything, and he believed she liberated France because it was even in the history books, but he was not sure he believed that she chose to be burned at the stake rather than deny her voices. The voices were from God, the book said, and so she died for the love of God. He wasn't sure he believed that anybody would be willing to die for God. Not in a fire. And he wasn't sure he believed that while she was burning she cried out "Jesus!" When you were burning, you just screamed. You couldn't cry out "Jesus" or "Daddy" or anybody. But Joan of Arc was a saint, of course, and that probably made a difference.

He thought about it for a long while, and he fell asleep thinking about it. When he woke up the next morning, he still wasn't sure how much he could believe, but he was sure of one thing. He would never be a saint if it meant going into the fire. Not for God. Not for anybody.

Maria looked up from her computer and listened. The elevator doors had opened and closed, but she hadn't heard anybody in the corridor. It was the silence that caught her attention.

She was working late again, typing a legal brief that one of her staff could just as easily have done. She stayed late at the office not because she had to but because it gave her an excuse for not going back to that house, to Ana Luisa, and to her son, whom she could not look at without crying.

She sat at the computer, listening. Everybody had left over an hour ago, so she was alone in this place. If it were the custodian, she'd hear the banging of wastebaskets and high-dusting poles and all his cleaning stuff. Besides, his cart had those squeaky wheels. But she could hear nothing.

She got up and went to the outer office and looked around. It was empty, and everything was just as it should be, except that the new receptionist, a girl called Velma, who chewed gum and wore too much makeup, had left a coffee mug on the corner of her desk. Office rules were very precise about this: absolutely nothing was to be left on desks overnight.

Maria scooped up the mug and bent down to put it in the bottom drawer of the receptionist's desk. She was still bending over when she became aware that somebody was standing in the doorway. It was a tall, thin black man, twenty or twenty-five. He had a close beard and he wore a tee shirt that said *Hard Rock Café* on the front. He just stood there, staring at her.

"I didn't hear you," she said. She moved closer to the desk. How did he get in here? How did he get past the guard downstairs? "That door is supposed to be locked," she said.

"It was open."

"Well, it doesn't matter," she said, "because we're closed."

He said nothing.

"You'll have to come back tomorrow," she said.

"I'm looking for somebody."

"There's nobody here," she said, and wished she hadn't. "Except the maintenance men and the guards, of course." She nudged the chair away from the desk and began, slowly, to slide the middle drawer open. She glanced down—paper clips and file cards and old phone memos—and then looked up at him.

He was still staring at her.

"You have to go," she said.

He took a step backward into the corridor and looked one way and then the other.

She yanked the drawer farther out and there, toward the back, half hidden in a mess of papers, lay the letter opener she was hoping to find. Her fingers closed around the handle, and with one quick motion she took it from the drawer and concealed it in the folds of her skirt.

She looked up at him, but he was gone.

She stood behind the desk, motionless, not knowing what to do. Then, slowly, she moved toward the open door and looked down the corridor to the elevator. He was standing there, his hands folded behind his back, looking at his shoes. Suddenly, at the far end of the corridor, the women's room door opened and Velma came out. "Sugar," she yelled, and went running to the man, who held his arms out to her. Maria closed the door and locked it.

She leaned against it, like somebody in a bad movie, thinking, What's happening to me? A guy comes to pick up his girlfriend and I think he's going to murder me. Still, why didn't he say he was looking for Velma? Why didn't he say *something?*

Quickly she crossed through her own office into Mr. Ackerman's, where she could look straight down to the front of the building. In a few minutes the door opened and the couple came out, Velma in a purple suit, the guy in jeans and a tee shirt. He had his arm around her.

Maria sat down and covered her face with her hands, the letter opener hard against her cheek. She began to shake.

In a moment, though, she pulled herself together. She was not going to give in to craziness; she'd had enough of that in her life. She was going to do something. She was going to save herself at least, since it was too late to save anybody else.

She got her bag and her coat, and on her way out of the office she dropped the letter opener into the receptionist's desk. Enough of that lunacy.

As she was crossing the parking lot to her car, however, something strange happened to her. She felt as if somehow she were suspended by strings—just ordinary strings—and far, far below her lay not the tarmac but the waves of a black ocean that she could fall into at any moment. It was like one of those out-of-

body experiences she had read about, where you're
still yourself but you're able to watch what is happening to you. And she knew, suspended from these long
strings, that if she looked down, she would fall, and
be lost forever. And she heard herself say, "So don't
look down." And, still aware of the danger, she fixed
her gaze on her car and kept walking.

She would refuse to think of John. She would just
put him out of her mind. It was five years since it had
happened. She wanted to start living again, and she
would.

In her car, she ran a comb through her short hair,
and shook it, and she put on fresh lipstick. She was
as ready as she'd ever be. She drove a short distance
to the Get Lucky Lounge, parked her car, and—she
was going to do this and she was not going to think
about it—she went inside.

The place was dark and smoky, and the rock music
was too loud. She paused inside the door and waited
till her eyes adjusted to the dim light. What the hell,
she said to herself, and moved through the crowd up
to the bar. A man turned to look at her. That was
good. If she was going to go crazy, she might as well
have some fun doing it. She wanted to laugh. She
wanted to scream.

"White wine, please," she said, and looked into the
mirror where she could see they were checking her
out. There were more men than women, and the
women looked pretty, but she could still hold her own.
She, at least, didn't look desperate—which was funny

when you thought about it because she was more desperate than anybody there. But in a different way.

"White wine," the bartender said, and slid the glass across the bar. She put a five-dollar bill next to the glass and pushed it toward him, but he just left it there.

She felt somebody at her back and as he bent toward her she could smell his cologne. It was expensive, like Mr. Ackerman's. She could feel his chest against her shoulder and she waited for what would happen. She could feel his breath at her ear.

"I bet you really want it," he said, playing the phantom lover. His voice was deep and full, even though he whispered. "I bet you'd love it."

She turned on the barstool to face him, and then she broke into laughter. He was short and thin and he wore granny glasses. Her phantom lover was a computer nerd. She laughed again.

"What's so funny?" he said, rattled, and he stepped back from her.

"You're funny," she said, "and I haven't laughed in . . . days."

"My name is Arthur."

"Yes, I want it, Arthur," she said, fixing him with her eyes. "Yes, I'd love it."

Arthur laughed too, then, and he held out his hand to her, and they left the Get Lucky Lounge together.

"My place?" he said, and she laughed again. It was good to laugh. It was good to be crazy.

. . . . .

An anonymous letter came addressed to Russell Whitaker, and after the prison authorities opened it, they decided to give it to him. A guard shoved it through the bars, and waited.

The envelope contained a newspaper clipping about John, and a picture of him celebrating his eleventh birthday. They called him the miracle boy. He had survived third-degree burns on eighty percent of his body, they said, and he had survived over a hundred operations as well. He was cutting a birthday cake and smiling at the camera. He didn't really have a smile; it was just a gaping hole with no real lips and no sign of teeth, but the caption beneath the picture said he was smiling. The last line of the article reminded the reader that John's father, Russell Whitaker, had done this to him. Russell Whitaker, it said, would be eligible for parole in just one more year.

Russell looked at the picture without any show of emotion, until finally the guard gave up watching and went away.

That night one of the jockers let himself into the cell and told Boyle to suck him off. Boyle refused. The jocker had bought him from Sharkey for two packs of cigarettes, so he slapped Boyle around a little bit, and Boyle pleaded with him to stop, and then finally the jocker got tired of Boyle's whining. He yanked him up off his cot and sat him down on the toilet and stood in front of him. "Now suck it," he said, "or I'll have to get rough."

Russell had been lying on his cot, deliberately deaf

and blind, thinking as always of his son, John. But suddenly he heard Boyle's voice saying Please and Please, and it was John's voice, and at once he was all over the jocker, punching and flailing, crazy with rage, and he did not stop until the jocker lay there unconscious.

After that, the word went around that Boyle was Whitaker's kid, and so they left Boyle alone.

At school, at home with Ana Luisa, in the hospital, John wanted only to read. It was as if the world he lived in was the pretend world and the one in books was real. At eight he had read all of Thornton Burgess, and at nine he went on to the Lone Ranger and the Hardy Boys and even Nancy Drew. Suddenly there was nothing left to read, and he watched television all the time, but it didn't take, and at ten he was back reading again. Now, at ten and a half, he had just finished reading *Catcher in the Rye* and *Robinson Crusoe* and *Jane Eyre*. He liked these books. They were about people like himself, who lived in secret.

When he was alone in the house and he was sure he would not get caught, he went into the bathroom and turned on all the lights and took off his clothes. He examined his face and body in the mirror, looking into his mouth, lifting up his new eyelids, and, with a hand mirror, examining his ears. He was not this person, he knew that. This person was Freddy Krueger. But then, who was he?

When he grew up, he was going to be a doctor like

Dr. Clark. He loved Dr. Clark. Dr. Clark always asked about the books he was reading.

He was reading *Wuthering Heights* now. If they ever made a movie of it, he would like to play Heathcliff. Heathcliff was exciting and mysterious, just like his father, that bastard.

Peggy was on night duty this week, and though it gave her a chance to catch some extra sleep, she missed talking with her patients. They never depressed her; their suffering was just part of the deal. It was like having a family, a big extended permanently wounded family, except they never turned on you, the way family did. It was easy to love them.

Especially John. He was back again for yet another operation to make that blob on his face look like a nose.

Tonight, when she'd finished her tour of the ward, she sat down by his bed and let her hand rest on his. In the darkened room, in his sleep, he turned his hand palm up and closed his fingers around hers and held on, tight, as if he were holding on for his life.

He was smart. He was tough. And inside him was this deep well of feeling that he never let out. When he did let it out, someday when he *could* let it out, it was going to be pure love, and it was going to be wonderful to see. She knew that. If he ever got the chance to love.

. . . . .

"I want to," Boyle said. "I want to do it for you."

"For Christ's sake," Russell said.

"I hated doing it for them," Boyle said. A long time later he said, "But I want to do it for you."

"Shut up and go to sleep," Russell said.

Boyle got out of bed and stood in the dark, looking into Russell's face. After a while Russell opened his eyes and sat up.

"I love you," Boyle said.

Russell punched him and there was a sick, cracking sound as his fist struck Boyle's jaw. Boyle let out a cry like a hurt rabbit.

"Don't ever say that to me," Russell said.

Waiting in chow line, Sharkey stabbed Russell in the eye with a fork. Russell wouldn't say who did it, so after his eye was looked at in the prison hospital, he was given two weeks in the hole to think about it. When they let him out, they discovered his eye was a festering mess, so he was sent to a real hospital to have it removed. He was there over a month with a series of infections, and afterward, because the prison would not pay for a glass eye, the hospital gave him a black patch to wear. They put him back in the same block, the same tier, the same cell.

When John was eleven he suddenly became interested in clothes. He had to have a 49ers sweatshirt, and Reeboks with foam in the heels, and jeans that were torn a little at each knee. He wanted the jeans that you bought already torn; when you tore them yourself, they didn't look as good.

One morning while he was getting ready for school, Maria looked in on him and told him to hurry up because Ana Luisa would be here any minute, and then she went back to her room to finish dressing. She was in the kitchen having coffee when she realized that John was still in his little alcove with the curtain pulled. She was about to shout for him to hurry up, but instead she got up and went quietly to the door and moved the curtain aside very slightly.

John was standing in front of the mirror, combing his hair. He combed it back straight and examined himself full face, in profile, and full face again. He combed it to the side and looked at himself critically, and then combed it to the other side. He turned and looked back over his shoulder. He smiled at his reflection in the mirror.

That was when he saw his mother standing at the gap in the curtain, watching him, spying on him as he looked at himself. She had seen him. She knew him now. He felt scalded. The blood rushed to his neck and face, tears pricked his eyes, and he shouted, "Get out. Get out of here."

John would not go to school that day and he would not say why. And he would not talk to his mother for nearly a month.

Nobody bothered Russell much anymore, but one day in the showers, just for the hell of it, a couple of the jockers decided to jump him. They got him from his blind side while he was covered with soap. One of them grabbed him by the hair while the other gave him a sucker punch that knocked him unconscious. Before they had a chance to rape him, though, a guard showed up and said, "Oh, shit mother, is he dead?" He wasn't dead, but they couldn't bring him around either, so the guard had a couple trustees carry him to the prison infirmary.

Russell was hospitalized for two weeks, and when he got back to the prison, they gave him two weeks in solitary for unprovoked attack.

John was twelve now and understood what was going on: his father was in jail for setting him on fire and his mother couldn't bear to look at him.

His grandmother drove him to school and picked him up every afternoon. She gave him his meals, bought him his clothes, took care of him after each new time in the hospital. She made him say a prayer every night. She was a pain in the ass, but she loved him.

His mother didn't care whether he lived or died, except when she was drunk. Then she always cried and hugged him and said she couldn't stand it. But when she was sober, she was out every night with Arthur.

He wanted to hate his mother, but he couldn't.

He hated his father though.

. . . . .

Dr. Clark was sitting opposite the shrink, just looking at him. They'd been like this for almost five minutes now.

"Why don't you ever say anything?" Dr. Clark said. "You never say anything."

"Like what?"

"Anything. Something."

Dr. Clark had been seeing this man, off and on, for a period of years, and he had nothing to show for it —except, of course, that he was still alive. But he'd come to an impasse today, finally. He was going to shut up. He was not going to say another word. He'd sit there till hell froze over or until the shrink said something, whichever came first.

Almost immediately, the shrink began to speak.

"All right, I'll say something about you." He spoke very slowly. "You are an intelligent, talented, sensitive man, but you want an unconditioned, unconditional love, invulnerable to loss or to change. You want it desperately. You want to give it and you want to get it."

The shrink stopped, waiting for the reaction.

"Yes?"

In spite of himself, the shrink laughed. "Well! You can't get that in this life. It doesn't exist. That's why man invented God."

Silence.

"You wanted me to say something," the shrink said.

. . . . .

"He's your son," Ana Luisa said, standing in the bathroom doorway.

Maria was putting on her lipstick, getting ready to go out. In the mirror, she looked hard at her mother, then finished with her lipstick and reached for a tissue.

"Couldn't you stay home with him, just this one night?"

Maria crumpled the tissue and slammed her fist against the sink. "I have to live too," she said. "I have a life, you know." She held her breath, trying to get calm, but when she turned to face her mother, she lost control completely. "Leave me alone!" she screamed. "Goddammit, leave me alone!" She snatched the water glass from the sink and flung it against the wall. It shattered with a sound like a gunshot, and bits of glass flew everywhere. "I can't stand it," she screamed. She flung open the medicine chest and began to pluck out everything inside. The bottles of pills, Band-Aids, mouthwash, scissors—everything went tumbling into the sink, the bathtub, onto the floor. "I can't stand it," she screamed, crying now, beginning to shake, beginning to come to the end of this little moment of despair. Soon she would bend over the sink, and sob, and shake some more, and then eventually it would be over.

Ana Luisa waited in the doorway, knowing all this.

John did not wait. He left the house and went next door to Ana Luisa's house and put on the television, loud. Then he got comfy in the big chair and began to read *The Wind in the Willows*. He had loved this book as a child.

The parole board was faced with a dilemma. If they let Whitaker out, the media would be all over the story and there'd be flak from every direction. On the other hand, there was no solid reason to keep him incarcerated any longer. His record was good. He'd been a model prisoner, more or less. And besides, the prison was hopelessly overcrowded.

"What have you learned from your time in prison?" they asked him.

"To stay alive," he said.

They nodded. They were sophisticated men and women. They granted him parole.

FOUR

In his dream, John was six years old again, and his father had come to see him. He leaned over John's bed and scooped him up and held him high in the air, at arms' length, pretending he could fly. "Who is my favorite little boy in the whole world?" his father said. "Who is that boy?" Pretending that they flew, he carried John from the sleeping alcove to the kitchen, ducking down to get through the doorway, zooming above the sink and the stove and the table, flying, then ducking through the doorway to the living room, flying everywhere, flying over the tables and lamps and chairs, flying until they collapsed together, laughing, on the living room couch. "It's Superboy," his father said, hugging him close, giving him kisses, being the way they used to be, before the fire.

Then his mother was crying. He tried to tell her it was all right, and he put his arms around her so she wouldn't feel so bad, but she pushed him away. He was in the hospital after that, with Dr. Clark and Peggy, and he was happy, but then he was home again and his mother was crying. He had to make her stop, because it was his fault she was crying. "Mother," he said. "Mama." And she stopped crying then. He tried to give her a kiss, and she let him, but when he pulled away from her, he saw her face, as if she couldn't stand to touch him. She felt bad about it, but she couldn't help it. And he couldn't change the way he looked. He tried to curl up and cover his face and cry, but his arm was in a splint and his hand was tied to the bed and he couldn't move his legs. Up in the corner of the ceiling was a small brown square, very heavy, and he had to concentrate on it so that it would not fall. And he would have to concentrate forever.

But it was summer, and he was twelve now, and all that was over. They were walking in a field of flowers, he and his father. The sun was warm. With each step they took, the long grass bent beneath their feet, and the daisies, pink and white, bobbed against their legs. In the distance they could see a hill of mustard flowers, and just over that hill lay the ocean. They were going to swim. They were going to play on the beach. But for now, they were walking in the field, together, and the sun was high, and there were flowers everywhere. They could, if they wanted, lean slightly forward, lift their feet from the ground, and fly. Skim across the field, above the flowers, soaring a little, dipping, lighter than air. Flying. But they walked instead, and the sound of the ocean grew loud and louder, and John took his father's hand.

They were together at least.
At least they were together.

Russell walked out of jail a free man, or so they told
him, but he knew that after what he'd done, he could
never be free again.

He had agreed to all the terms of his parole. He
was forbidden to have contact with his former wife or
child; he could not visit San Jose without the knowledge and permission of Forte, his parole officer; he
must check in with Forte each morning and each evening; and he must wear—day and night—the transis-
torized ankle bracelet that allowed them to monitor
every movement he would make for the next three
years.

He could live with his father, the parole board said.
At the time of Whitaker's release, the father was still
living within the San Jose city limits, but he had agreed
to relocate and provide a home for his son. He'd be
a good influence, they felt, since he was active in AA
and was himself a reformed alcoholic. He could provide the stability and family support that ex-convicts
so badly need.

Forte, through connections, even got him a job with
a painting contractor.

Russell pretended to be properly grateful.

"Now listen up," Forte said. "I've got troubles of
my own, and I've got seven parolees to watch out for,
so I don't want any shit off you. You slip even once

and you're back in the joint. Got that? So no going
near your kid or your ex, that's first of all. And, second
of all, keep your ass out of San Jose. And, third of all,
don't hang out with known criminals, and you'll be
okay. Okay? But you miss one check-in with me, or
go one inch off the straight and narrow, or we catch
you playing with even one match, and I myself personally will get a blowtorch and apply it to your dick.
Capisce?"

Russell understood. He would be the model parolee,
he said. Straight and narrow. No blowtorch.

He had fifty dollars and a terrible new suit. He took
the bus as close to his father's house as he could get
and then walked the rest of the way. His father was
home, and after they had said hello, Russell took the
keys to his father's car and drove slowly past Maria's
house and then past the special school and then past
the hospital where John had been cared for by that
doctor. He circled back to Maria's house again. And
then he went home.

He would never be free, he knew.

The media were in an uproar when they learned that
Russell Whitaker, the child-burner, had been paroled
sometime during the past week.

Why had it all been done in secret? they wanted to
know. What community was he in now? What name
was he living under? Who would he burn next? TV
reporters and newspaper reporters and local stringers
from the *Star* and the *National Enquirer* swept down

on San Jose, on Maria's house and Ana Luisa's house, on the Burn Unit, on John's special school. They were everywhere. They wanted names and dates and facts. They wanted pictures. They wanted them now.

As it happened, they got nothing about the Whitakers.

What they got instead were pictures of the earthquake.

A plate of rock beneath the ocean shifted a few inches, moving north, and another plate shifted to accommodate it, moving south, and then they settled down and everything was much the same again. Except above, in San Jose, where buildings rocked on their foundations and trees shook and for twenty seconds everything stopped, completely silent, completely in balance. Walls gave way, fires broke out, cracks opened in the street. People tried to run. They screamed. They panicked. And then, with a hard sigh, the Central Overpass collapsed, pinning cars and their drivers beneath tons of steel and concrete.

It was not the Big One. It was only a seven pointer, but it made great pictures and it made a great story.

And it pushed the Whitakers out of the news, completely.

Forte put a green X next to Russell's name each morning and evening, and once or twice he checked the monitor to make sure Russell was at work, but beyond that he almost never gave Russell a thought. He had got him a job as a painter or a carpenter—he didn't always remember which—with no complaints so far, and God knows he had plenty other things to think about.

Money, for one. During the earthquake his house had shifted on its foundation, not so badly that it fell apart but badly enough so that he could never get insurance on it and he sure as hell couldn't sell it. So he was stuck with this piece of shit. He'd bought it in 1970 for $30,000 and he'd been about to sell up for $650,000 and retire at sixty to the Bahamas, but now it wasn't worth diddly-squat and he'd have to keep on working forever. For shit wages. Besides, that blond bitch was running around on him again; she was only forty-five, and she was all legs and tits, too young to be tied down, she said. And to be honest, he himself was back on the bottle, a little bit. So who had time to worry about Russell Whitaker?

Forte poured himself one last drink.

He had enough to worry about, thank you very much. That dizzy girlfriend. His house. Early retirement. And a bunch of ex-cons who were *real* problems. Druggies mostly. One rapist. One killer. Russell Whitaker was the least of his worries.

At Ana Luisa's house all the glasses tipped over on the shelf, dishes fell out of the cupboard, and everything in the medicine chest tumbled into the sink. Nothing broke. And the shrine of the Virgin Mary survived intact. Maybe it wasn't a miracle, but Ana

Luisa thanked the Virgin anyway. These things were
beyond our understanding.

For Emory, the earthquake was only another event
that failed to interest him. What drove him back to
the bottle, and nearly killed him, was his son, Russell.

Russell had moved in and taken over. According to
the terms of Russell's parole, they were supposed to
move out of San Jose, but when Emory reminded him
of that, Russell had said, "Forget it." In the same way
he'd said, "I need the car at one-thirty this afternoon.
Make sure it's here." In the same way he'd said, "I'm
living here now. You can stay or leave, but I'll need
the car." It was the way he said everything, and it left
no room for argument. He had become a very scary
man. It wasn't just the way he talked. It was the way
he held himself, the way he moved, the way he looked,
especially with that eye patch. He lived out on the
edge of some precipice. He was a man who had nothing to lose.

"You're violating parole," Emory said to Russell.

Russell was reading the paper.

Emory said, "You're not supposed to even *be* in
San Jose."

Emory said, "You're following that woman, aren't
you."

Emory said, "The boy—"

Russell stopped him in midsentence. He held up his
burned hand, and Emory looked at it, and fell silent.
Russell turned back to his newspaper.

Emory went to his bedroom and tried to say the rosary. He tried to read the AA book. He tried to concentrate on his higher power. Nothing worked, and so he went to the bathroom and fished out his emergency bottle. Just a sip. And then, surprising himself, he put the bottle back.

He went out to the kitchen and looked at Russell, big and lumbering and stupid. Who did he think he was? He thought he ran this place.

Emory could feel the need for a drink burning inside him. As if his brain were on fire.

"Listen," Emory said. "I want to talk to you."

Russell stood up, his hands at his sides.

Emory looked at him.

Russell looked back.

"What do *you* know about pain," Emory said, and he spat on the floor. He wiped his mouth and was about to continue, but Russell looked so big and so angry that Emory forgot what he wanted to say. He got his wallet and a heavy coat for nights and the hunting cap he always wore when he went on a bender. He let himself out of the house and, mechanically, as if he had no choice in the matter, he set out walking for the nearest bar. And then he would hit the next. And the next. Until there was no more pain at all.

John was about to get in the car with Ana Luisa, when suddenly he changed his mind. He put his books on the front seat and said to her, "I'll be back in a minute, Gram," and then he walked slowly toward the car that

was parked across the street and down a little from
Ana Luisa's. As he approached it, a man got out and
turned toward him, waiting.

John stopped a short distance away and stared at
him.

"You're my father, aren't you," he said.

Russell looked at him squarely for a moment, and
then he nodded his head. He did not speak. He wore
a patch over his right eye.

"You've been following me," John said.

Russell nodded again and looked at him, longingly.

"If you come near me, you'll go back to jail, you
know. If you even follow me and *don't* come near me,
you'll go back to jail. I know that. I know all about
you."

Russell continued to look at him.

"Why don't you say something? I'm not afraid of
you." He stood with his fists clenched, facing his father. He wanted to say one more thing. He wanted to
make him suffer. He wanted to kill him with it. But
he could think of nothing except 'I hate you,' and that
sounded too childish. And so he said nothing.

He turned around and walked back to Ana Luisa's
car. He scooped up his books and sat with them in
his lap, staring straight ahead.

"What did your father say?" she asked.

"Nothing."

"And what did you say?"

"Nothing. I told him I could put him in jail for
following me. I told him I knew all about him."

"He's a poor sinner, like the rest of us," Ana Luisa said. "But keep away from him."

"I hate him," John said, and he could hear the sound of hatred in his own voice. He wished he had said it to his father, that bastard. It didn't sound childish after all.

They drove home in silence.

Ana Luisa had been shocked by the sight of Russell. He looked old and beaten. She had read in the paper about the stabbing in jail, the loss of his eye, the beatings, and she'd been prepared for a criminal or a madman. But he was just pitiful. She was not afraid of him at all. In a strange way, she felt bad for him. He had been crazy, out of his mind, and she understood that.

She glanced over at John, who sat there silent, his eyes slitted. His beautiful eyes, in that ruined face.

There was no explaining what Russell had done, and no justifying it. It was from the devil. But it was done now, and they all had to live with it. In a way she didn't understand, she accepted it as the will of God. Poor John. Poor Russell. Poor everybody.

Before they got out of the car, though, Ana Luisa said to John, "If he tries to talk to you again, Juanito, run away from him. Run away fast."

Suddenly she had an inspiration that made her feel a lot better. "Someday," she said, "I'll take you to the shrine at Altamira. Then you'll understand."

Forte hadn't begun his serious drinking yet this evening, and he was in the mood for a chat.

"So tell me about work," he said. "How's work going."

"Fine," Russell said. "I'm lucky to have that job."

"Luck, shit. I got you that job and don't you forget it."

"Right."

"Painting, is it?"

"It's a great job."

Forte squinted to see if he could detect sarcasm. "So, you keeping your hours, Whitaker? Clocking in and out on time?"

Russell nodded. He did not mention that he clocked in at 7:00 A.M. and out at 1:00 P.M. and, moreover, that he had the top boss's okay for this. In his first week on the job, he'd explained to the super that from 1:30 to 3:30 each day Forte had work for him on another job site. When the super demanded to know where this job site was, Russell shrugged and said to check with Forte, that it was a private thing, a personal thing, that Forte wanted some work done on his house or something. The company had hired parolees before, and the super understood at once that Forte and the top boss had made some kind of deal, so he simply cut Russell's pay and said to hell with it, it was no skin off his dick. And Russell was free every day at one o'clock.

"Keeping away from that kid?" Forte asked.

"Away from the boy and away from San Jose," Russell said.

Forte looked at him, hard.

"I swear to God," Russell said.

"Good, good," Forte said. "You just keep your nose clean." He was tired of chatting now, so he opened his file drawer and took out the bottle of bourbon and the glass. "And remember, with that bracelet on your ankle, you're under surveillance every minute of every day."

"Sure," Russell said. "You bet."

Forte waved him out and started in on the bourbon. He didn't trust Whitaker. He didn't trust any of them. Parolees were just convicts on leave from jail, no more, no less. Liars and cheats. Scum.

It was a mystery to him how people always managed to fuck up their lives.

Maria's car was in the garage for a tune-up, and they'd found extra work that needed to be done on the transmission, so Arthur was meeting her at six at the Get Lucky. They'd have a drink or two, a quickie at his place, and maybe some dinner. Then he'd drive her home.

But she wasn't in the mood for dinner. She wanted to get home to John. She wanted to watch TV with him, or make popcorn, or just sit around and be a family.

"Well, let me come too," Arthur said.

She thought for a while.

"I can watch TV with the best of them," Arthur said. "I can make popcorn, if it's microwave. What do you say?"

"You haven't seen him," she said.

"I've seen his picture. In the paper."

"It's not the same," she said.

They had been meeting each Friday—not dating, really; just drink, dinner, and bed—ever since that crazy night in the Get Lucky when he'd leaned into her and whispered, "I bet you really want it." It was the first time he'd ever done anything like that. It was her first time too, and they hit it off so well that they kept on seeing one another until the day her son's picture appeared in the newspaper and Arthur realized who she was—the ex-wife of that lunatic and the mother of that pitiful, burned-up child. He skipped the next Friday at the Get Lucky. He went to Touch-down instead and tried his terrific line on someone else—who slapped his face and threatened to call the cops—and in a couple weeks he was back with Maria. He had missed her, and not just the sex. He began to think he loved her, maybe. At any rate, he felt bad for the child.

"So let's go," Arthur said. "We'll watch TV, eat some popcorn. I'll be nice to him."

"You don't have to be nice to him," she said. "He's not a charity case, you know. He's quiet, but he's very, very smart."

"I can handle it," Arthur said. "I'm sort of smart too."

"Just treat him the way you'd treat any twelve-year-old."

"I will. I will." He slipped his arm around her shoulder.

"And don't be touching me. He's not used to a man in the house."

"I won't touch you and I won't be nice to him. I'll just be normal. And smart."

But, despite the newspaper photo, Arthur was not prepared for the way John looked. He had expected scars and a dented nose and some trouble around the mouth, but in fact the boy's face looked as if they hadn't finished putting it together yet. It was still in pieces. The newspaper photo, it turned out, had been very kind.

Maria introduced them, talking too much and too rapidly, and then she started to prepare dinner.

"I had dinner at Gram's," John said. He sat down and looked at Arthur, watching him carefully.

Arthur could think of nothing to say.

Maria glanced over at them as they sat there, silent. "You two just sit down and relax," she said. "I just have to wash this lettuce and heat the casserole."

"We *are* sitting," John said.

"And we're relaxed," Arthur said.

It was very quiet in the kitchen. The clock ticked. Maria ran the water and then turned it off. The refrigerator clicked on and began to hum.

"How about I make us drinks?" Arthur said. "Okay? G and T for you, Maria? What'll you have, John? You can show me where the stuff is." He started looking for glasses. "Right?"

Here he stopped for a moment and looked straight at John, frankly, as if he were merely asking a question.

John looked back at him.

Arthur flinched, but kept on looking.

"Okay," Arthur said, defeated, and went about making the drinks. "Okay. All right. Here we go." And eventually they were seated across the table from each other once again. "So, John," he said, "tell me about school."

"It's a special school," John said. He paused for a second—and his mother turned and gave him a look—but he did not say, "for freaks," as he usually did.

"What about sports? Do you play sports, John?"

"Baseball."

"I hear you're very smart," he said, staring at John.

John was caught off guard, and looked away.

From the moment they'd met, John had not taken his eyes off Arthur's eyes. It was a new trick of his, and he knew it was not very nice: testing people to see how they reacted to his face.

"Are you, John? Very smart?"

"Arthur!" Maria said. "Never mind him, John. He's just being rude."

"Psst! Hey, John! Are you?"

"I read a lot," John said, "and I'm articulate. That's what Ms. McGill says. She says that's not the same as being smart."

"Well, you seem very smart to me, John."

"Thank you," John said, and the pink patches on his face seemed to go red.

Arthur reached out as if to touch him, but then drew back.

"Have you read *Great Expectations?* Dickens?"

Arthur laughed. "John, you're out of my field," he said.

"You're an accountant, I know that," John said. He looked down, embarrassed. "I just thought you might have read it."

"No, I haven't read it. But why don't you tell me about it. Go ahead, John."

John thought for a while and then he said, "Why do you say John all the time? How come you say my name when you're talking to me?"

"Maria," Arthur said, laughing. "You've gotta help me out here. This kid is too smart for me."

Maria laughed, and Arthur laughed some more, just a tiny bit too much.

"It seems I have a talent to amuse," John said. He had read this in the school library during lunch hour, and it came back to him now, so he said it. Sarcasm. Arthur was making fun of him, and his mother was on Arthur's side, so he had a right to be sarcastic. His father wouldn't make fun of him. His father wasn't silly, and he wouldn't laugh just because somebody else laughed.

John stood up and said, "Arthur? I have to do my homework, Arthur." And to Maria he said, "I'll do it at Gram's."

Later that night John lay awake in bed, going over what he had said. He'd been a show-off and he'd been sarcastic. "I read a lot, and of course I'm articulate, Arthur." What a little shit he'd been. He wondered if Arthur would marry his mother and be his new father. He and Arthur could go to baseball games together. They could go to the beach. Watch TV. They could be a perfectly normal, ordinary family. But he didn't want Arthur. He wanted his father. His father had looked straight at him and hadn't flinched, even for a second.

Maria, too, lay awake, going over the evening. Arthur had been good. He had tried. And John had tried too, in his way. But how could she think of any future, with Arthur or anybody else? This is how things were: she was going to be John's mother for the rest of her life, period, and there was no sense crying about it.

Still, if only . . .

She hated to think it, ever, but tonight she could not help herself.

If only she could be free.

Russell trailed Maria and found out about Arthur. To his astonishment, he discovered he felt nothing.

Because she wouldn't love him, or couldn't love him, Russell had nearly burned his son to death, and now, when she loved somebody else, he found he just didn't care.

He cared only about his son. How could he ever make it up to him?

The door to the examination room opened, and there was Peggy. She threw her arms around him in a big hug. She kissed him and he kissed her back.

"John!" she said, "you old apple pancake, you!" She touched his face and neck, smiling. "You're looking so good," she said. "Those grafts have taken beautifully, don't you think? And they'll look even better in a year or so. And your hair! I'd kill for hair like that!" Peggy went on, just saying things to make him feel good, and he did feel good, because what she meant, really, was that she loved him. He knew it didn't count, because she was a nurse and not somebody in his real life, but it was nice just the same.

"I've got a new glove," he said, and held out the baseball glove he carried everywhere with him.

"From Gram?" Peggy said.

He nodded, rubbing the leather with his thumb.

Then they talked about baseball and school and the books he'd been reading and what he wanted to be when he grew up. He wanted to play second base for the Giants, he told her, and she said, You will, I know you will, and then suddenly she leaned forward as if she were going to hug him again, but instead she gave him lots of little punches on the arm. "You look so *good,*" she said, laughing, "I could just eat you with a spoon." She checked her watch. "I'll get Dr. Clark for you, Johnnikins, and I'll see you before you go." In another second she was out of the room.

John sat on the examining table and waited. He

loved Peggy and he loved visiting the hospital for his checkup. Peggy was the only person he ever kissed, except for Gram. His mother had tried to kiss him once, but he had pulled away from her when he saw the pain and fear in her eyes. She didn't want to kiss him. She was just forcing herself to. He would love her because she was his mother, but he would never kiss her.

He put on his baseball glove and flexed it open and closed. He reached for a high one, got it, and drove his balled fist into the glove. A good stretching exercise, Dr. Clark had said. The baseball glove was his idea. Embarrassed suddenly, John put down the glove and waited.

There was a knock at the door, and it was Dr. Clark. He looked the same as always, except he was wearing a suit instead of his white coat, and he had dark circles under his eyes. He smiled in that little way he had, and he shook John's hand. "So how're you doing?" he asked.

"Fine," John said, annoyed with himself because he sounded like a child.

"Fine, fine," Dr. Clark said. "School okay? Tell me about school."

John was not doing very well in math. He liked the computer a lot, and he liked English class—Ms. McGill especially—and he liked history, but social studies was kind of boring and science was the worst. Apart from baseball, what he liked most was just reading.

John was sitting on the examination table and Dr. Clark sat in the patient's chair, looking up at John as he talked. The grafts had taken well, he could see. Good movement in the neck and throat. The ears looked fine. The scars were fading. Everything had been salvaged—except the boy's life, he thought. Another success. Another triumph for the art and science of medicine. His little smile turned ugly. He shifted in his chair, leaned forward, listening again.

"Tell me about your reading," he said. "What's your favorite book? Tell me all your favorite books."

But John had noticed the change in him and said nothing.

"You okay?" Dr. Clark said.

John met his glance and then looked away.

"What is it?" Dr. Clark said. "If you want to tell me."

"I saw my father," John said.

Dr. Clark nodded.

"I hate him," John said.

"Well, he hurt you, badly."

"Yes. And I hate him."

"Do the others know you've seen him? Your mother? Your Gram?"

John shook his head. He opened his mouth to say something, and then said nothing.

"Go ahead. It's all right."

"Can I whisper it?"

Dr. Clark stood up and leaned over the examination table, his face turned away, his hand cupping his ear.

"Why did he do it to me?"

Dr. Clark pulled back, shaken.

John made his voice even smaller. "Was I a bad boy?"

"You're a good boy," Dr. Clark said firmly. "Don't you ever think that. You're a good, good boy."

John's face went hard, and he withdrew into himself, but Dr. Clark scooped him up in his arms—to hell with decorum—and said, "You're a good, good boy. You're a good boy. You're a good, good boy."

Ana Luisa sat in the waiting room and prayed to the Virgin for guidance. Should she tell Dr. Clark that Russell had been following John? He'd go back to jail for sure. He was in violation of his parole. And he had done this terrible thing. Still, he looked so old and so beaten. She had watched in her rearview mirror as he stood beside the car talking to John, and she could tell he meant no harm. He wanted forgiveness. He wanted to be punished. She understood that. But if he wanted to be punished and he violated his parole, why *not* send him back to jail? He *should* be punished. But he had only one eye. And what did you do in an earthquake if you were in jail and had only one eye? "*Virgen Santísima,*" she said softly, "my little darling Virgin, tell me what I should do."

At once she knew what to do. If Dr. Clark came out to the waiting room, she would tell him about Russell. Dr. Clark would know what to do. If the nurse was with him, it would be a sign, and she wouldn't tell him about Russell. She had made up her mind. She stared at the door, expectant.

On the other side of the door, Dr. Clark was making rapid calculations. If John's mother was in the waiting room, he'd call her inside and tell her about Russell. If John's grandmother was there, and she probably was, he would . . . what would he do? Let the moment decide?

He opened the door to the waiting room just as the door from the hall opened and two men entered the room, a recovering acid burn and his Healthcare driver. Ana Luisa looked startled. She turned to the newcomers and back to Dr. Clark, and then she smiled at Peggy, who appeared directly behind Dr. Clark. "Doctor," Peggy said, and at the same moment he was paged on the intercom, and John turned back to shake his hand, and Ana Luisa came forward to say something, and everything stopped.

Dr. Clark put up his hands, surrendering.

"Help," he said.

Everybody smiled at everybody else.

The next day Russell followed John, and spoke to him, as they feared and knew he would.

"I knew you'd be here," John said.

Russell sat in the car and said nothing.

"Gram will be here in a minute, you know. She knows you follow me. I told the doctor. Everybody knows."

Russell nodded.

"How come you do it?" He leaned into the car on the passenger's side. "Is it because you're sorry for what you did to me?"

"Yes."

"Well, why don't you say it?" He waited. "Why don't you say 'I'm sorry'?"

Russell looked at him for a long time. "I am sorry, John. But that isn't enough."

"Can I get in the car?"

"Yes."

He got in the car but left the door hanging open. He was perched on the seat, half sitting, ready to run. "I'm not afraid of you," he said.

"No. I wouldn't hurt you. Never."

"But you did. You tried to burn me to death."

Russell nodded.

John wanted to kill him. He said, "My mother goes out with a man. His name is Arthur. She might marry him, and I hope she does."

John said, "They're in love. She doesn't love you anymore. She hates you."

John said, softer now, "*I* hate you too. I hate you more than anybody in the world. And you can't do anything about it."

"No," Russell said.

John punched him then. In the arm, as hard as he could. And again. And again, with both fists. He knelt on the seat and punched Russell in the chest, the neck, the face. He dented the black eye patch. John punched, and he kept on punching, until Russell's lip began to bleed and there were tears on his face. In all this time, Russell had not once turned away from the blows, not once lifted his hand to protect himself. John punched until he was too tired to go on.

He scrambled out of the car then, and slammed the door hard. "Bastard," he screamed. "Sonofabitch."

He was still shaking with uncontrolled anger—one of the crazy fits he sometimes had—when Ana Luisa pulled up in front of the school.

Ana Luisa told Maria and, despite John's howls of protest, Maria called the police. It's about Russell Whitaker, she explained, and in less than a minute they had connected her with Forte, Whitaker's parole officer. For some reason, Forte seemed angry at *her,* and he rambled incoherently as if he'd been sleeping or maybe even drunk.

Nonetheless Russell was arrested that evening at home. He came quietly, without any protest, even when his hands were cuffed behind his back. They led him out, and one cop pushed his head down as the other one helped him into the squad car. Next door, Janelle watched from the front step and her mother watched from inside the screen door. As the car drove off, Janelle turned and shook her head sadly, and her mother shook hers in response. It was too bad.

At the police station, however, Russell would not deny he'd been following John, but he would not admit it, either. "We have proof," they said. "Your electronic tag."

Russell smiled, because everybody knew those things malfunctioned all the time.

"Other people have complained," they said. "Your mother-in-law. This Dr. Clark."

"Whatever the boy says," Russell said.

"You can kiss your ass goodbye," they said. "You're dog meat, One Eye. You'll never see the outside again."

"Whatever the boy says."

"He *says* he hates you. He *says* he never wants to see you again. Can't you understand that?"

"If that's what he says."

"Besides, it's the condition for your parole. You can't have contact with any of them. Can't you get that straight? You've had it, pal. You're done for."

In the end, though, they let him go. The boy denied he had ever seen his father. He had made it all up, he said. He'd been lying. No, he'd never seen him. No, he'd never even seen his car. He insisted on it, he swore, he went completely out of control. They didn't believe him, but they had to pretend to take his word for it, because the mother had no proof, and neither did that Dr. Clark, and the boy's grandmother said she might have made a mistake after all.

They told Russell that if they ever got proof he violated his parole . . . well, he knew what to expect.

They told Forte that he'd lucked out on this one, but the next one meant his job *and* his pension *and* et cetera.

They told Maria that she'd better keep an eye on

that kid. She was playing with fire, they said. Get it?
But they were embarrassed for saying that, so they said
take care, lots of luck, have a good one.

During her lunch hour Maria went to mass at Saint
Anne's. She hadn't been to mass in years, and she was
distracted by the informality and the handshaking and
all the chatter, but she managed finally to think about
what she'd come here to think about. Russell.

Did she want him punished still more? He had lost
an eye, she knew that. But he still had his face, didn't
he? Which was more than her son had. Was it vengeance she wanted? And more and more vengeance, like
the Jews and the Arabs? Or was she just trying to
protect her son from his sick father?

The more she thought about it, the more confused
she got. She knew why Russell had hurt John. For her.
To get at her. To make her love him. And she knew
—but how did she know?—that John was safe with
him now. Russell would never harm him again. Russell
had given her up. He had replaced her with John.

Her mind wandered. She could see a time when
John would be all better, his face normal, and he would
decide of his own free will to stay with his father, who
would love him and take care of him and everything
would be good again. And she would be free.

The bells rang at the consecration, and she buried
her face in her hands. Christ was on the altar now, in
the bread and wine. My Jesus, mercy, she said to herself, and almost at once she thought, What nonsense.

How could she ever have believed such things? She sat back in the pew and examined her nails. She waited for a bolt of lightning to strike. Go ahead, she thought, strike me with a thunderbolt. Strike me dead. At least then I'll be free.

But by the time mass was finished and she left the church, she found herself praying, Just let me love him. Just let me love him enough. She meant John, of course, and so she was surprised to find she was thinking of Russell.

What she needed was Arthur. What she needed was sex. When she got back to her office, she called Arthur and made a date for right after work. She began to feel better at once.

Sex would be her salvation in the end.

"I'm going to Billy's house," John said, "so you don't have to pick me up after school."

Billy was a friend, another burn victim, and Maria was relieved that John finally had a friend. He needed friends. She was glad for him. More than a month had passed since the police incident, and there had been no sign of Russell anywhere around the house or the office or the school, but still she didn't trust him. Or John, either, for that matter. She was suspicious.

Ana Luisa was more than suspicious. She was convinced that John's friend was really Russell.

She parked around the corner, and when school let out, she was surprised and pleased to see John and Billy come down the path and get into a long gray

Mercedes. The car drove off, and Ana Luisa returned to her own car, relieved, and a little guilty. Poor John, she thought. Poor Russell.

An hour later, in west San Jose, John came down the path from Billy's house and got into his father's car and they drove off in the direction of the beach. They had two hours together. Father and son.

It was that easy.

John was fascinated by Russell's house, by the fact that Russell had lived there when he was John's age. Every time he visited, he explored the bedroom, he looked into the bureau—only blankets there—and into the closet, where there was a pair of shoes, some trousers, a few shirts, and a bright blue suit. He lay down on the bed and pretended he was his own father.

This afternoon they sat in the living room eating pizza and watching TV. There was nothing on except talk show stuff, but John didn't seem to mind and so Russell didn't mind either. They were watching Oprah.

Russell pretended he was not looking at John, but in fact he studied him the whole time. John was small for his age, and he looked frail, but he was strong and wiry, with a good, sturdy body and a wonderful mind. He was quiet, mostly, but when he spoke, he was quick and witty and smart. And he had fierce determination. Russell could see that whatever John decided to do, he would do. Nobody would stop him.

Everything he saw in John was a discovery, a revelation. The way he walked, the way he listened, the way he held his fork, ate, drank, the way he smiled, the way—like his mother—he leaned forward when he explained something. And he had Maria's eyes too. Maria's way of laughing.

Russell shifted on the couch, as if he were trying to get a better view of the TV.

He could see only traces of himself in John—the shape of the face, the strong chin. His son.

He wanted to devour him. He wanted to worship him. He wanted to kiss the child's feet and beg his forgiveness. But he could never ask that. He would never ask that.

Suddenly John said, "How come you always stare at me?"

"Do I?" Russell said. "Do I always stare at you?"

"All the time," John said. "How come?"

"I guess because I'm your father. You're my son." With forced casualness, he said, "I love you. So it's natural for me to stare."

"You're always staring," John said, frowning, but he sounded pleased.

Russell thought, This is the happiest moment of my life. These are the happiest days of my life.

Russell pitched the ball and John hit him grounders. John had a sharp eye and a good batting arm and he connected solidly with the ball.

It was a Saturday in November.

They were at the beach.

Russell was living his whole life over in John, and this time it was a good life.

They were walking through a field of mustard grass. It was February, but the sun was hot and there was no breeze and the yellow flowers stretched ahead of them for nearly a mile. John paused, and a long black snake slithered past him, and then they went on. John was not afraid of snakes. But Russell's heart beat faster, faster, and for a long time he said nothing.

Maria was late and Arthur was getting impatient. And then suddenly she was there, looking out of breath, as if she'd been running, as if she couldn't wait to see him.

"Sweetie," she said, and gave him a big kiss. Not a long one, because they were in the bar of the Get Lucky, but a big one, with lots of love, with abandonment, he figured. He let his hand slip lower on her waist, and he pressed hard. "Arthur," she said, "I'm sorry. I *am* sorry, really, but I can't stay. I've got to work late. All right? Okay?"

"I'll wait," Arthur said. "Then we'll go to my place."

"I can't," she said. "It's John. I've got to get home for him."

Arthur pulled a face.

"I do," she said.

She said, "Try to understand. Okay?"

She said, tired of being nice, "Forget it, Arthur."

Arthur hadn't had time to adjust to each new mood,

and he watched, confused, as she left the bar. He swung around on the stool and, blushing, said to the bartender, "Hit me again."

Maria never had time for love these days. Not even for sex. Work came first, she said. And then John. Arthur shrugged. Fuck that. Where was he supposed to fit in? After everybody else?

It was funny: for a while he'd been afraid of getting too involved because he wasn't ready for anything heavy yet, and because of the kid and all the bills, and because he liked his independence. And during all that time, she'd been hot for him, she was all over him. Then he went to her house for dinner that time, and met the kid, and found out the bills were taken care of by her health plan and by private donations and by this Dr. Clark, and he thought, Why *not* get involved? She was beautiful and sexy and, the big thing, she made him feel like he was a tiger in bed. He began to really fall for her. He was in love. And all of a sudden she began to pull back.

The problem, he realized, was that she didn't love him the way he loved her. She liked the sex, that's all. The only person she really loved was that kid of hers. John. A smart little bugger with a face like Halloween. How could she love that kid? How could she look at him?

"Hit me again," he said to the bartender.

Everybody, *everybody* was all fucked up.

．．．．．

Rain had begun to fall, one of those cold February rains that promised to go on forever.

Maria came in stamping the wet from her shoes. She tossed her umbrella in the sink, let her raincoat fall to the floor, and swept John into her arms, dancing with him across the kitchen floor. He laughed, and she laughed with him, and then she put him down.

"You're getting too heavy for this," she said, squeezing him hard. "My big boy. My wonderful big boy." She looked at him, and he was laughing and laughing.

"What?" she said. "What's so funny?"

"I'm just happy," he said, and threw his arms around her.

"It's a perfect night for popcorn," Maria said. "And a movie. And we'll turn up the heat."

But John was not listening to her. He was thinking that this was the first time she had ever looked at him without that pain in her eyes, and he was happy, happier than he had ever been in his whole life.

Dr. Clark, at his shrink's insistence, had been taking long walks. Walking was good exercise, and good exercise was good therapy, and blah, blah, blah.

Today he was doing the three miles around Lake Lagunita, an abandoned reservoir that had been tarted up as a kind of inner-city park. It was a very pleasant place. Mothers with babies gathered there each afternoon, and the joggers used the track in early morning and late evening, but at noontime it was a nice private place for a three-mile walk. And it was only a short drive from the Burn Unit.

Dr. Clark was feeling good today, he had a lot of energy, and to prove to himself that things were looking up, he decided to jog—from here to the live oak on the far side of the lake. Less than a mile. He felt funny jogging in dress shoes, Guccis no less, but the air was clear today and there was a cool breeze and for once he didn't feel like committing suicide. He was jogging well. His breath was strong and regular, and he fell into an easy stride. He could do a mile. Maybe more than a mile. But by the time he got to the live oak, he was winded and he slowed down to a walk. He stopped and rested, his hands braced against his knees.

As he stood there, bent over, a little dog appeared from nowhere. It was a beagle, or at least part beagle, and it stood ahead of him on the path, wagging its tail, a tentative look on its face. "Hello, you," Dr. Clark said. The tail wagged furiously, but the dog stayed where it was. "Come here," Dr. Clark said, squatting down, "come on." The dog crept toward him, its head lowered as if it expected to be hit. "Good boy, good fella." He rubbed the dog's chest and scratched behind its ears. The dog had no name tag, no collar at all. Dr. Clark stood up, and the dog raised itself on its hind legs, wanting more pats. "Walkies," Dr. Clark said, and set off again on the path, the dog by his side.

It would be nice to have a dog. He could get up early and walk it, and take it out for a run at lunch, and it wouldn't be much trouble. It would be good company. Also, there were professional dog-walkers —he'd seen them, with five and six dogs at a time— if he had to go away for a conference.

He looked down at the dog and, as if it knew it was being watched, it looked up and wagged its tail. Dr. Clark laughed out loud.

I've got a dog, a beagle, he imagined saying to the shrink. He could see the shrink's surprise. And how do you feel about that? the shrink would say. I think it's good, he'd say; I *feel* good about it. I'm not afraid that it will die, or run away, or burn. It's just a dog.

"You're a nice little dog," he said aloud, and stopped to give him a pat. The dog stopped, too, and looked up expectantly, and Dr. Clark froze there, with his hand above the dog's head. He stopped, frozen, because he saw not the brown and white dog with its head tipped up, expectant, but a brown and white dog with its four legs spread out and strapped to a board, a slit from its throat to its pelvis, and wires leading from a machine to its heart and back again, for an electroshock experiment. The dog convulsed, the heart beat wildly, and the little lights on the machine blinked as the essential data were recorded. And the high, thin scream of the dog—who had no feelings, they said, not like us, not like human beings—went on and on.

Dr. Clark stood and looked out over the water. After a while he started walking again, and when he got in sight of his parked car, he said, "Go away," but the dog kept with him. He stopped and pointed back to where he'd first seen the dog. "Back," he said, his voice hard. "Go!" He stamped his foot. The dog cringed and backed away. Dr. Clark turned and began walking more rapidly toward his car. The dog followed at a little distance. In a minute Dr. Clark looked back, saw the dog, and stamped his foot again. "Get out of here," he said. "Go! Go!" He began to walk faster, and then to run, and finally he was at his car, fumbling with his keys. The dog stood far off by the lake, looking at him.

Dr. Clark got into his car and drove back to the hospital, doing forty-five in a thirty-mile zone, refusing to think, refusing to feel anything. He would never have a dog. He would never have any living thing.

John always made sure to spend an hour at Billy's house before his father picked him up, so that when his mother or his grandmother asked him where he'd been, he could say honestly—more or less—that he'd been with Billy. Today Billy was showing him jewelry he swore he had stolen from Barker's House of Gems. He had a man's ruby ring with a Stanford crest on it, a white and black bracelet with a gold clasp, a pearl necklace, and a little locket on a thin gold chain. He spread them out on his bed for examination.

"You didn't steal these," John said.

"Did."

"You're full of shit."

"Fuck you. I did."

John thought for a minute. "Give me one."

"I *did* steal them."

"Give me the locket."

"Not unless you admit I stole them."

If he stole them, it was from his mother and father. But John wanted the locket, and so he said, "You stole them. Okay? Now give me the locket."

"I'll trade you."

"No, you've gotta give it. You said I had to admit you stole them first, and I did, so now you've got to give it."

Billy put his loot away, one thing at a time, until only the locket was left, and then he gave it to John.

"Okay," John said, "now what did you want to trade it for?"

"What've you got?"

"I've got shit. What do you want me to trade you?"

"I'll have to think."

"Fuck you, Billy. You tell me now, or you don't get anything."

John didn't care what Billy asked for. His father would get it for him and he'd pass it on to Billy. The important thing was that he had a nice present for his mother. A gold locket. He'd put a picture of himself inside it. The one from his sixth birthday. The last one taken before the accident.

"I'm thinking," Billy said. "Wait a minute. Wait a minute."

"You must believe *something*," Peggy said. "You must have hope? Right?"

Dr. Clark had asked her to come have a drink with him, and then he'd dumped all this stuff on her. Depression. Despair. Maybe even suicide. And before this they'd never even had a personal conversation. She could have died of embarrassment.

"But think of the wonderful work you do. Surely that must—you know—give you something to live for."

"I believe nothing. I hope nothing. My work is just work."

Peggy took a sip of her drink and put it down again. She had to say something meaningful. Something to help this good man, this good doctor, a saint, really. She took another sip of her drink and then pushed it away, all business. She surprised herself by what she said.

"You've got to get a grip," she said. "You're just feeling bad for yourself. Think of that kid John. Think of his *father*. How'd you like to be one of them? Get a life. Go dancing, for God's sake." She shot a quick look at her watch. "I'm late," she said. "Gotta go. Got a hot date." And she left Dr. Clark sitting there in the bar.

It was days before she could look him in the face again.

. . . . .

John opened the package excitedly, tossing the ribbon aside, tearing at the paper. It was exactly what he'd asked for, a Stanford sweatshirt, white, with *Stanford* printed across the chest in red. He tried it on.

"It's too small," John said.

"It's a medium," Russell said. "It fits fine."

"But it's supposed to be loose. It's supposed to sort of droop." They were in Russell's bedroom. John was standing in front of the mirror, and he looked up and saw Russell's expression. "But it's fine," he said. "Maybe after it's washed it'll get bigger."

"Come on," Russell said, and they got in the car and drove up to the Stanford bookstore and bought another sweatshirt, large.

Again John stood in front of the mirror. The sweatshirt was much too big. "Perfect," he said. He turned to face Russell, shy suddenly. "Thank you," he said. "I'm going to leave it on."

They went into the living room to watch TV. Something was tickling the back of his neck, and John reached around, fiddling blindly, until he brought out the pin that held the price tag there.

"A pin," he said. He shifted on the couch until he was leaning against his father. They were watching a western, with Clint Eastwood. John turned the pin over and over in his hand.

"Thank you for the present," John said.

Russell put his arm around the boy's shoulder and patted him.

"How come you always give me presents?"

"Because you're my son and because I love you."

He had found it easier to say as the months went by.

"Do you really love me?"

"You know that."

"Are you making it up to me? For what you did?"

Russell didn't say anything for a while, and then he said, "Nothing can ever make up for what I did."

John stuck the pin idly into the sofa cushion and then, idly still, pressed the point through the knee of his trousers. He felt a sting on his kneecap. It did not feel like a pin.

"But would you make up for it if you could?"

"We shouldn't talk about this, John."

"But you would, wouldn't you? If you could?"

A long time passed, perhaps a minute, while the only sound in the room was the television. Then Russell said, "I'd give my life for you, John."

John snuggled up against him. He rolled the pin between his thumb and his forefinger, he stuck it lightly into his knee, he held it between his lips. Then he sat up straight and, leaning forward, he took Russell's hand in his own. He turned it palm up, and held the index finger out straight. He took the pin and placed the point of it very lightly against the pad of his father's fingertip. He pressed the pin. The skin went white. He looked up into his father's face. His father was looking back at him. Without taking his eyes off his father's eye, John pressed the pin harder, a little harder. His father blinked, but he said nothing and his face did not change. John looked down, and he could see a dot of blood forming where the pin pressed. He looked back at his father and pressed again. There was no change in his face. John looked at the pin and could see it had sunk into the finger— he wondered how deep?—but still there was only a drop of blood. He wanted more blood. He wanted his father to beg him to stop. He pressed harder, looking at the finger, and the pin seemed to go so deep that John could feel the pain himself, not in his finger, but in his chest. He looked up, and there were tears in his father's eye, but his expression was still the same, and he was only looking. He was not angry or pained or anything. He just looked sad.

John pulled out the pin and ran to the bathroom and returned with a wad of toilet paper. He pressed the tissue to his father's finger, squeezing it to get the blood out so there would be no infection, and then he wrapped the finger in the paper. In a minute a dot of red appeared. John went back to the bathroom and found a Band-Aid. He concentrated on the finger, and he did not look up at his father's face.

When there was no more sign of bleeding, John said, "I want to go home, please. I want to go now."

Russell drove him home. They rode in silence, and John did not say goodbye when he got out.

But that night John cried himself to sleep.

Russell did not cry. He lay in bed, shaking. He shook, convulsed, with the cold knowledge of his help-lessness. He would give anything, even his life, if that would help the boy now. But nothing would help. What you destroyed, you could never make whole again.

And so, what could he do?

Ana Luisa had been out dancing, but it just wasn't fun anymore. Maybe she was getting too old. The men were clumsy, they were pigs. And she had this ache in her chest. So why not go home and have some nice wine and watch a little TV?

She got home well after midnight, but the lights were on next door, so she went around back and tapped on the kitchen window. John came to the door, a book in his hand.

"*Poquito,*" she said, and gave him a kiss. "You're up so late. You read too many books."

"*Les Misérables,*" he said. "It's kind of boring, actually. Would you like a beer? We don't have any wine."

"I hate beer," she said, and made a face.

John got her a beer and poured it into a tall glass. "So where is your mother this time of night?"

John smiled.

"Arturo? Or another one?"

"There have been quite a few since Arthur."

"*Pobrecito.*"

"Well," he said, imitating, "she has to have a life too."

Ana Luisa looked at him.

"She's not dead yet, you know."

"What are you saying, Juanito? What do you mean?"

Out front, a car pulled up, and they heard a door slam.

"Here she is," John said.

Maria came in, locked the door behind her, and turned to face them. They were sitting at either end of the kitchen table, just looking at her.

"Well, what?" Maria said.

John said nothing.

Ana Luisa looked up at the clock.

"So it's almost one," Maria said. "So what?"

"I didn't say a thing."

"God!" Maria stormed into the bedroom. They could hear her slamming things around in there, and then suddenly she was back, wearing only her slip. "I have a life too, you know," she said. "I'm not dead yet." She went into the bathroom and slammed the door.

"See?" John said. He took his book and went into the little alcove and pulled the curtain. He was going to read in bed.

The fight would go on for a long time, he knew.

An hour later, when his mother and grandmother had shouted and screamed at one another, and said all the mean things they could think of, they cried and made up and it was all over. They hugged each other, and then Ana Luisa went home and Maria went to bed. It was quiet in the house. It was quiet all up and down the street.

John lay in bed, still wide awake, thinking that he would see his father tomorrow. His father would do anything in the world for him. Anything.

Emory got out of detox, but he did not have the courage to go home. This had been the longest binge of his life, or at least the longest since he'd joined AA.

He was sober again, and he could remember how it began—with Russell's return from jail—but there were whole weeks since then that remained a blank. Where had he been? What had he done? Had he attacked Russell? Tried to burn his hand? Or was that Ana Luisa, the one who used to cook for him? And how long had he been gone?

He walked to the nearest homeless shelter and, by sheer luck, he got a bed for the night. The next morning—more luck—he got a one-day job packing dishes for a moving company. He was still shaking pretty badly, but he broke only a plate and two cups, and nobody seemed to care so long as the stuff got packed. They gave him forty bucks. He ate at Burger King and went to a flophouse for the night.

In another week or so—if it was a good week like this one—he'd be ready to go back to his AA group. And once he'd faced them, he'd be ready to face Russell. Maybe.

Dr. Clark had been a Catholic once and, thinking about where he could turn next, he discovered that nothing much was left except religion, so he decided to give it one more try. On the morning of Good Friday, therefore, he arrived at the Trappist monastery above Point Reyes to make a three-day retreat.

The liturgy was beautiful. He was moved by the chanting of the monks as they sang the Office. And the monastery itself, a stone building on a stone cliff, took his breath away.

He found himself tempted once again, despite everything, to confide in someone. The shrink had proved hopeless, of course. Big surprise. And when he'd tried to confide in Peggy, she had put him— firmly—in his place. What he had felt as despair seemed to her no more than self-pity, and her brisk down-to-earth response over drinks had made him see that sometimes despair *was* self-pity. But he was smart enough and fair enough—even to himself—to realize that he was becoming immobilized, that he could no longer feel as a normal person, no longer function as a competent surgeon, and that this was not self-pity but something final and fatal.

What he feared was not death, but this living death.

On Holy Saturday he surrendered to temptation. It was evening, and the singing at First Vespers had brought him close to tears, and he was hungry and sick. He entered the cloister and walked down the long stone corridor until he found a door ajar and a light inside. He tapped softly and pushed the door open wider. The tiny cell was barren, with only a crucifix on the wall, and for furniture a cot, a green metal desk, and a kitchen chair. A very old priest sat at the desk with his hands folded in front of him. He was not reading or saying his beads. He was just sitting there, with a purple stole in his hands and a kind of smile on his round red face. He had very thick glasses, tinted pale blue.

When he saw Dr. Clark in the doorway, the priest shook out the thin purple stole and put it around his neck, ready to hear confessions. He motioned Dr. Clark to sit on the edge of the bed.

Dr. Clark sat down. "This isn't confession," Dr. Clark said, too loudly, and then he repeated himself. "I don't want to confess; I just want to talk to someone . . . for a minute."

"What a fine voice you have!" the old priest said. "You could sing opera. You could sing on the television."

Dr. Clark leaned forward, his elbows on his knees, and it all came pouring out. "I'm becoming paralyzed," he said, "because I see what people do to one another. A boy burned by his own father. And not a crazy man, just a man. People sicken me. I can't look at them. *Flesh* sickens me. The cruelty, the rottenness. Even a dog I saw, I saw it flayed, cut open, and it looked at me. I can't *not* see. There is this little boy . . ."

He went on to the end, a rambling hysterical account of the cruelty he saw everywhere around him, paralyzing him, ripening him up for suicide.

The old priest listened, his eyes attentive behind the pale blue glasses, as if this account of despair were new to him. When Dr. Clark finished—and it took him a long while—the priest said, "What a good man you are! And what good vision you have!"

Dr. Clark shook his head, exhausted, not really listening now that he was done.

"You see things as they are, of course, and that can't be changed. We're a cruel and horrible race of men. And women too, of course; they're cruel too. And horrible. It's all just as you say."

He took a deep breath, and for a long time said nothing. He had rather hoped Dr. Clark might listen, but he knew how these things went. You couldn't tell what was going on inside. He started in again, his voice higher and lighter.

"But we aspire sometimes—some of us—to love. Sometimes even our cruelty grows out of love. It's too awful, isn't it, and too mysterious. But we *aspire,* don't you see? And sometimes we love."

He leaned forward and lowered his voice, as if he were imparting some special message, as if this alone mattered: "What makes life so horrible," he said, "is that our salvation never comes in the form we would have chosen."

"Do you see that?" the priest said.

And he said again, "You do see that? God sanctifies us—he makes us saints—in his own way. Not in our way. It never looks like sanctity to us. It looks like madness, or failure, or even sin. We don't know how we stand with God, and we want to know. We want some evidence that we are loved, that we are saved, but all we have is our own darkness, and God's darkness. But sometimes, in that darkness, there is a single act of love, some selfless gesture, an aspiration, and we see that it's not been all waste, all hopeless, and we can . . . well . . . go on."

He leaned back, drifting off into his private thoughts, and for a long time there was silence in the little room.

"That's why you shouldn't kill yourself," the old priest said, folding his hands. "But that's my opinion only, and what do I know?"

Dr. Clark looked up, finally. He had not heard a word. But he was startled, because the priest was looking at him in a funny way. With admiration, almost. He blushed as the priest continued to admire him.

"Did I miss something?" Dr. Clark asked.

"You're like an angel, who sees too much, I think. You see things as they are," the priest said.

"An angel," Dr. Clark said.

"If an angel came to earth, I imagine he would see things as you do. Or she, of course. But right now I'm considering a male angel, you see, you understand. An angel would see evil as evil, and corruption as corruption, and the stink of rotting flesh would make it suicidal, I have no doubt. *We're* immune to all that. Our humanity is a kind of immune system all by itself. But the angel would have no immune system, nothing to protect its pure spirit from the realities of this world. It would see things as they are. And it couldn't live."

For no reason he could think of, Dr. Clark suddenly

thought, Peggy is out dancing now. Getting picked up, maybe. Getting laid for Easter. Like an egg.

"You're like an angel, I think."

The priest reached out his hand and placed it on Dr. Clark's shoulder. The hand was heavy and warm and protecting. Dr. Clark looked up into the old man's eyes.

"It's possible, of course, that you're just a lunatic. But I think not. I think you are an angel."

Despite himself, Dr. Clark laughed, a short barking sound.

The old priest laughed too, but faintly, as if he were laughing at something else.

"For your penance say three Hail Marys and do one nice thing for yourself." The priest slipped into Latin then, reciting the formula of absolution.

"But this wasn't confession," Dr. Clark said. "I didn't want to go to confession."

"Go in peace," the old priest said.

At the door, Dr. Clark turned and said, "What nice thing?"

The priest took off his stole and looked at him.

"You said, 'Do one nice thing for yourself,' and I wonder what nice thing I should do?"

"What a funny man you are," the priest said and, smiling, returned to the contemplation of his folded hands.

Dr. Clark went away too exhausted to think. None-theless he did think. Was the man mad? Was he dangerous? 'I think you are an angel.' Good God, the whole world was insane.

He lay down for a minute and fell asleep immediately. He slept straight through the night, missing the entire Easter Vigil and the sung mass on Easter morning. When he woke, he felt a great deal better than he had in a long while.

A little less angelic, he said to himself. And a whole lot less shitty.

They had spent the day together at Great America, and John rode the roller coaster so many times—death-defying, the thrill of your life—that the man who sold tickets told him not to ride anymore because he'd get sick, but he sold John the admission ticket anyway. He proved to be right; John got sick and threw up in front of the ticket booth. They left after that and drove home to Russell's house.

Emory was watching from behind the curtains. He saw them get out of the car and go around to the back, and when he heard the key in the lock, he let himself out the front door and disappeared down the street, walking. He'd been out of detox for three weeks now, but he was still not allowed in the house when John was there.

Inside, John went to Russell's room and lay down on his bed. He fell asleep immediately.

When he woke, he stretched and found that he felt good. The pain in his head was gone, and his stomachache was gone, and his father was sitting there beside the bed.

"Daddy," John said. "Papa."

It was just beginning to get dark.

John let out a little laugh. He was in one of those moods. Sometimes when he was with Russell, when everything was going nicely and he was feeling happy and close to him, as if the burning had never happened and they had been just father and son all along, sometimes, without any warning at all, he'd suddenly get the urge to be mean, to hurt him, to make him prove he was sorry, and to make him prove he loved him. He didn't know why this happened, and he was ashamed of it, but there was no resisting it, and now, once again, he rolled over on his side and gave in to it.

"With your eye patch, you look like a pirate," John said.

"I am a pirate," Russell said. He held up his burned hand. "Captain Hook." He hadn't meant to say it, it had just slipped out, but after a second or two John laughed.

"You're funny," he said. "That's funny."

He sat up on the bed and bent closer to Russell. "Put on the light," he said, "so I can see your face."

Russell put on the light.

"Lean closer."

Russell did.

John put out his hand, tentative, and then he

touched the eye patch. It was hard, like cardboard or plastic. Russell did not move.

"I want to see," John said. "Underneath."

"John, no," Russell said.

"Yes."

"You don't want to see that. It's ugly. It's just a wound." Nonetheless he began to slip the stretch band off his head, from back to front—he couldn't stop himself—until the eye patch came away. There was angry red flesh underneath, and a dark hole.

John brought his face up close to Russell's. "I can't see," he said. "Move closer to the lamp."

"John, no," Russell said, but he moved his chair closer to the lamp and tilted his head, exposing the wound for examination.

John knelt on the bed and leaned close to the light. He tilted Russell's face at an angle, and with his thumbs, he gently pulled and pushed the loose flesh away so that he could see deep into that hole. The skin twitched beneath his thumbs, and he pressed harder. The flesh rolled all the way back and the empty eye socket was exposed—pink, and purple, raw. Nothing else. John was dizzy suddenly and lost his balance. He fell against Russell and Russell supported him, but John continued to examine the socket. What had he expected to see? He closed the wound, gently, with his thumb and forefinger, and then he put the eye patch back in place, and slipped the stretch band back over his father's head. Shaking now, a little frightened, he took a quick glance at his father's face. It was sad, but there were no tears.

They looked at one another, frankly, and they were ashamed. What were they doing? Where could they go after this?

Russell took John out to the car to drive him home.

Crouched down behind an abandoned car, Emory watched them as they drove away. He was filled suddenly with a sense of loss. Not the kind of loss he felt when his wife died, or that other, different loss when he first hit bottom and reached out for AA. This was something else altogether. A nagging ache, a warning of some terminal pain that would surely find him, no matter what. Because at last there was no place to hide.

Everyone sensed that something was about to happen. It was inevitable. It was like fate. But nobody knew what it would be, or where, or when.

Forte thought he knew. He phoned Russell six times in one day. Each time he found Russell on the job and hard at work, except for the last time, when he was at home, just as he was supposed to be. During the following week, Forte continued to phone him on the job at least twice a day, until finally the super told him to give it a rest, they were trying to get some fucking work done around here, and if Forte was so worried about Whitaker, why didn't he just put him in jail? Forte thought about that and afterward phoned only once a day.

Ana Luisa thought she knew. She went to bed each night expecting an earthquake, and she was surprised each morning to find herself alive. Even before she washed her face, she went out to the living room and knelt before her little shrine to offer a prayer of thanksgiving. She said a special prayer for Maria. She said a whole rosary for John. She even stopped in at a noon mass one day, but she had not been to mass in years and she was uncomfortable with all the English and the handshaking—as if everybody else had come to a party and she was there to spy on God. She left almost at once. Later, when the church was empty, she went back and prayed. She lit a candle. "Protect us from evil," she said to the Virgin, though she had no idea what the evil might be.

Dr. Clark knew something terrible would happen every minute of every day. Nonetheless he had asked Peggy to show him how to dance. It was just an experiment, he insisted, just this one time. So they were having a drink and a quick dinner before she took him up to the city to hit the clubs.

"To dancing," he said, and held up his wineglass. Awkward and uneasy with this strange man, Peggy clinked her glass against his and said, "To dancing and to good times and to . . ."

Both were thinking, To John.

Peggy felt a moment of panic, and Dr. Clark, panicked too, clinked his glass a second time, hard, and the wine sloshed onto the tablecloth.

"To the good life," he said, shaken.

"To the good life," Peggy said.

And for a moment neither said a thing, as John's life rose before them, very briefly, and then sank out of sight.

"You're gonna love to dance," Peggy said, "I can tell."

"I'm gonna try," Dr. Clark said.

They laughed, at nothing, but it was important to laugh, and after a while they forgot about John and had a very good time. Dancing was not so bad after all, Dr. Clark felt. Better than a pointy stick in the eye. Better than suicide.

Everyone—except Maria—sensed that something was about to happen. Maria felt nothing. She went to the office each day and she worked late each night. She knew that Ackerman wanted to replace her: she'd let him down; she was always distracted. But what could she do? She had to live too. Sometimes after work she met a man. Sometimes she just had a drink with him. Sometimes she had a drink and they went home to his bed. A different man each time, if she could manage it. She wanted no permanent involvement with anybody, not Anglo, not Chicano, not anybody. She needed work and she needed a little sex and she needed to get through this life somehow. She could never marry again. She was John's mother, period, for good. There was no point in hoping for anything better than that. Or easier.

Still, she had to have something. Some kind of life. She was not dead yet, you know. And so she saw men, she went home with them, and who was going to tell her that she couldn't? Who would dare?

It was Saturday night and Maria was getting dressed to go out. She went back and forth from the bedroom to the bathroom, first in her robe and curlers, then later in her slip and heels, and finally with her hair combed out and her makeup complete and her earrings on. No necklace. No bracelet. No Mexican debris. She was all set except for her dress.

Ana Luisa sat at the kitchen table, watching all these trips back and forth through the kitchen, frowning, puffed up, letting Maria and John and the whole world feel the force of her disapproval. John sat opposite her, pretending to read.

Finally Ana Luisa couldn't help herself.

"Maria," she said softly.

"Don't start," Maria said. "I'm going, and that's that."

"Of course you are, *querida,* of course you are. But you'll be home early, won't you? For the boy."

"Yesss." She disappeared into the bedroom and returned almost immediately in her new black dress. She was fiddling with the zipper in back.

"Maybe you could stay at home tonight?" Ana Luisa asked. "What do you think? For the boy."

"I'll be home early, I said. Now leave me alone." She turned her back and said, "Help me with this, Mother, will you?"

"So lovely," Ana Luisa said, zipping the dress up

and fastening the tiny clip. "You look like a little dream."

"I'm *going,* Mother."

She stepped into the bathroom to check her makeup one last time. She needed a touch more lipstick.

She could tell they were looking at her, both of them, but she was damned if she'd respond. John hadn't said a word, the little tyrant. He knew the power of his silence.

She turned her head slightly and caught John in profile, his hand to his chin, as he read his book. And suddenly she saw him transformed. He was no longer this burned and patched little boy but the handsome son she had always dreamed of—serious, smart, bent over a book. John Whitaker.

In that instant she was overcome with the fear that something might happen to him. It was more than a fear, it was a realization—something *would* happen, she knew it—and she sprang to him and hugged him hard against her breast. "My sweet," she said. "My precious son. I love you. You know that. I love you."

He pulled away, embarrassed, and then saw the look on her face and the tears, and he hugged her back.

"I love *you,*" he said.

"What a silly I am," she said, hugging him one last time, and then she went into the bathroom to repair her makeup.

At the table, Ana Luisa covered her face and said nothing.

John read his book.

Russell picked him up at ten the next morning. Maria was still asleep—she had come home around dawn— and so John left her a note on the kitchen table. "Dear Sleepyhead," it said. "I've gone to the beach with Billy and his folks." To piss her off just a little bit, he signed the note *Juanito*. But then he felt bad and added: "P.S. A Christmas present, early." And he left the little gold locket lying next to the note. There was no picture inside, but she'd find something to put there.

Without a word John got into his father's car and they drove off in the direction of the beach. It was a beautiful sunny day, but as they got nearer the coast, the sun disappeared and the fog began to roll in.

They stopped at Nini's Place for coffee.

"How's my boy?" Russell said.

John just smiled. It wasn't a question that needed an answer.

They had said almost nothing to each other so far this morning. They had driven in silence over the Santa Cruz Mountains, and they were silent now, but it wasn't one of their old, comfortable silences. This one was charged with expectation, and they both knew it.

The waitress was a gum-snapper. She took Russell's order, and John's, and then walked away without ever having looked at them. In a minute she returned with the coffees and, sliding them across the table, she caught sight of John's face. She stopped chewing for an instant, and caught her breath, and then she said,

"You all enjoy it now." She snapped her gum again, loudly.

John had seen her.

Russell saw him seeing her.

There was nothing to say.

Back in the car, Russell began to hum, a little nervous. "Do you still sing, John?" he asked. "You used to sing all the time. You had a nice voice, like your mother's."

"My voice is changing," John said.

"Will you sing for me?"

The question hung there for a long minute, and then John said, "Yes." He began to sing "Silent Night," and though his voice cracked when he got to "Sleep in heavenly peace," he went right on through the three verses he knew. His voice was high and pure.

"Nice," Russell said, trying to sound casual.

John sang "Joy to the World" and "God Rest Ye Merry, Gentlemen," and he began "O Holy Night," but the range was too high and he gave it up.

"See?" he said. "My voice is changing."

Russell put his hand on John's head for a moment and then ruffled his hair. Neither said anything.

They were near the beach now. The fog had cleared, and the sun was high in the sky. It was going to be a sunny day after all.

Russell drove past the beach they usually went to and continued on down the coast. He went past places he had gone to with John, past others where he'd gone with Maria, past one place where he had sat alone, often. Finally he stopped at a long field, with a hill beyond it. They could hear the surf pounding just over the hill.

John took his baseball and glove and got out of the car. There was no path, but they started out walking any which way, side by side, in no hurry. They were walking in a field of flowers, he and his father. The sun was warm. With each step they took, the long grass bent beneath their feet, and the daisies, pink and white, bobbed against their legs. In the distance was a hill of mustard flowers, and just over that hill lay the ocean. They were going to play ball on the beach. If it got warmer, they might go for a swim. But for now, they were walking in the field, together, and the sun was high, and there were flowers everywhere. If this were a dream, they would simply lean forward, lift their feet from the ground, and fly. But this was not a dream. It was much better than a dream. John took his father's hand.

On the beach they tossed the ball back and forth for only a short while. Neither was interested in playing anymore. They were impatient for what was to come, as if they knew, as if they had planned it all along.

At two o'clock they were back in the car, still worked up from running on the beach but, somehow, shy with each other.

"How about a Big Mac?" Russell said. "A shake? Double fries? What do you say?"

John shook his head.

"Would you like to go to a movie? The mall? A video shop?"

"No," John said.

"Well, what then?" Russell waited, and when he spoke again, his voice shook. "Do you want to go home? With me?"

"Yes," John said. "I want to go to your house." He felt immensely powerful, and cruel, and just. He felt like God or the devil, it didn't matter which one. "I want to lie down on your bed."

Neither said anything until they reached Russell's house. Then John took a quick glance at the front window and said, "He sees us, so he'll be gone in a minute." They went around to the back, and as they entered the house, they heard the front door close. Emory was safely out of the way.

John lay down on the bed.

Russell stood at the doorway, waiting.

"I'm not sleepy," John said.

"No," Russell said.

John looked at him for a long while. "You said once that you would do anything for me."

"Yes."

"Do you remember that? To make it up to me, you said."

"Yes."

"Would you?"

Russell nodded.

"Anything?"

Silence.

"Anything at all?"

Again Russell nodded. He couldn't look at his son. He knew what was coming, he too had laid plans for it, but it was obscene, it was sick. But it was also just. And he knew that.

"Will you set yourself on fire? For me?"

"Yes?"

"The way you did it to me? On this bed? With gasoline?"

"Paint thinner."

"Will you? Now?"

Russell went out to the car and got a gallon can of paint thinner and came back to the house. John had taken off the bedspread and the blanket. He was standing by the door, waiting.

Russell sprinkled the icy fluid from the head to the foot of the bed and then back again. When the can was half empty, he turned it upside down and let the stuff soak into the pillow where his face would be. He kept on pouring until the can was empty.

He couldn't look at John.

He lay down on the bed. "Now?"

"Now," John said.

Russell reached into his breast pocket where he had the matches ready, but before he struck one, he looked at his son and said, very softly, "I want you to *know* I love you."

He struck the match.

John was on top of him at once, smothering the tiny flame, clutching the dead match in his fist.

"I'm sorry, I'm sorry," John said, and he said it again, louder, more out of control, and then he began to scream. Russell held him close as John screamed himself into exhaustion, and he continued to hold him as the boy shook, convulsed, as if he could not stop crying. But he was not crying. It was a choking, gasping sound. The ache, the betrayal, lay too deep for crying.

Russell held him until he was quiet.

After a time John got up and stood beside the bed.

Russell, too, got up. He gave his son a hug, but he said nothing. There were no words.

They were standing in front of the bureau, avoiding each other's eyes, when suddenly they discovered they were looking at each other in the mirror.

"That's us," Russell said, and he smiled.

John smiled too, studying his father's face, and then Russell saw the boy study his own face, and he saw the smile tighten, and he saw something in John's eyes go dead.

"Let's go," he said. His mind was made up.

Russell opened the car door for John, and then he went around and got in the driver's side and pretended to be confused for a moment. "I forgot my keys," he said. "Wait here, John. I'll be right back."

He jogged around the house to the back.

John sat in the car, his head bent forward, trying

not to think of what he had almost done, but thinking of it anyway. He had nearly burned his father to death. He had asked his father to do it, and his father had spread the paint thinner and soaked the pillow and lay down on the bed. He would have done it. He would have lit the match. And it would have been John's fault.

He loved his father, but he had never said it to him. Deliberately. It was the last bit of power he could hold over his father, he knew that. He could hold his love back to the very end.

But he wouldn't hold it back. He would do it now. He would say 'I love you' as soon as his father came back with his keys.

"I love you," he said aloud, just to hear the words, and as he said them, he realized his father had not left his keys behind—he'd opened the car door, after all —and he'd gone back to the house, to the bedroom, to that bed, and now John would never see him again.

John flung the car door open and ran to the back of the house. The door was locked. The key was gone from the ledge above the bathroom window. "No," he shouted, and pounded on the door.

He went back to the bathroom window, but it was locked, and so he hit it with his fist until it broke. He hoisted himself up onto the sill, fell back, and tried again. This time he made it, though he cut his hands on the broken glass, and in only a minute he pushed himself through the window and tumbled onto the bathroom floor. It was then he heard the whooshing sound, an explosion of flames from the other room, and he heard his father's low moan.

He was at the doorway and his father lay in the bed, in flames. He could run away, he could save himself, but he only stood there, watching. He knew well what it meant to burn. He knew exactly what he was doing. And then, with a terrible cry, he plunged into the fire. "I love you," he said. And he cried out, "I love you."

The flames were slow, and not merciful.

Later, when the fire was out and the corpses carried away, the medical examiners had trouble separating the two bodies. Their arms were tight around each other, and their chests had melted together, and there was no recognizing the faces. But everyone knew who they were. Everyone had been expecting something like this. It was just one of those awful things that happen.

THE
PILGRIMAGE

A year passed, and then most of another year, before Maria's transformation was complete. She was transformed in personality and character and—finally—in soul, a change so absolute that nobody seeing her would recognize the old Maria. In her living room she had a little shrine to the Virgin and she prayed there each time she left the house and came back, before each meal, whenever she was tempted to complain. Around the statue of the Virgin she had placed photos of her mother, her dead husband, her dead son. There were talismans too: a wedding ring, a note from her son folded tight and slipped inside a locket, a pair of joke glasses.

Physically, the change was even more dramatic. She had become an old woman—impossible to guess how old—a Hispanic peasant lady who cleaned houses and spoke very little English and visited the church each morning and each night. She dressed like her mother, though not so well, and she worked alongside her mother, and she lived with her mother too. They fought continually.

Long before her transformation was complete, Maria had planned her pilgrimage to the shrine at Altamira. She had a map, and she had plotted out the roads they would follow, the distance they would cover, the time it would take . . . to walk from their purple house in San Jose to the shrine at Altamira.

Walk? Was she crazy? Her mother would have nothing to do with it. Maria begged, insisted, taunted her. Finally she threatened to go by herself, and then her mother gave in.

They had been walking for almost a week when they reached Point Reyes, and it took a full day, and then another, before they could locate the shrine. Maria stood alone among the tall cypresses and prayed to the Virgin Mary, Mother of Hope. "Forgive me for what I ask," she prayed. "Forgive me for what I do," and then she tacked her little sheet of paper to a tree and read it through yet again to make sure she had said it right.

Holy Mary, how is it you permit such things? My son burned, and then my husband burned, and then my son burned again and forever. I know it is God's will. I know I must accept it. But I ask you now, and I will ask you at the day of judgment, I will raise my voice before the throne of God and shout and will demand an answer: Why?

Two lines beneath, in her small neat hand, she had written "Why?" It was signed *Maria*.

The note hung there for a day and a night, and then the hard winds that blow through Altamira tore it free, it was rained on, it was nibbled by deer. Someone found it eventually—an old priest or maybe an old drunk, what difference does it make?—and saved the last remaining scrap, and tacked it once more to the tree. All that remained was the single word "Why?" and the name *Maria*.

From what, the pilgrims wondered, had she been saved?